Shiloh

When Martha Pootes watched the three Union soldiers
approach her parents' farm in Kentucky, she had no inkling
of the stark horror they would bring. Raped and all but dead,
the young woman manages to impart a very sketchy description of her attackers before breathing her last.

Returning to General Grant's Army of the Tennessee, the
men believe that they are in the clear. Unfortunately for
them, Martha's uncle just happens to be a deputy United
States marshal. Knowing only that one of the rapists has a
powder burn under his right eye, the marshal joins Grant's
forces. But being part of an invading army means that not
only is he in mortal danger from the fugitives, there is also
the very real risk that in pursuing them, Pootes could be shot
by the Confederates defending Fort Henry on the Tennessee
River. And that's only the start of it all!

By the same author

Blood on the Land
The Devil's Work
The Iron Horse
Pistolero
The Lawmen
The Outlaw Trail
Terror in Tombstone
The Deadly Shadow
Gone West!
A Return to the Alamo
Taggart's Crossing
A Hell of a Place to Die
Death on the Bozeman
Bone Treasure
Western Union
Lords of the Plains
The Forgotten Land
Tears of the Buffalo
North of the Line
Reign of Terror
Texas Fever

Shiloh

Paul Bedford

A Black Horse Western

ROBERT HALE

© Paul Bedford 2020
First published in Great Britain 2020

ISBN 978-0-7198-3079-2

The Crowood Press
The Stable Block
Crowood Lane
Ramsbury
Marlborough
Wiltshire SN8 2HR

www.bhwesterns.com

Robert Hale is an imprint
of The Crowood Press

Typeset by
Derek Doyle & Associates, Shaw Heath
Printed and bound in Great Britain by
4Bind Ltd, Stevenage, SG1 2XT

AUTHOR'S NOTE

Nathan Bedford Forrest was widely considered to be the foremost general of the American Civil War on either side. And he was in a Confederate Army that contained such outstanding individuals as Robert E. Lee and Thomas 'Stonewall' Jackson. He reached the rank of lieutenant-general and, amazingly for such a senior officer, was wounded four times, personally killed thirty-one men and had thirty horses shot from under him. At the end of the war he said that he was 'a horse ahead'!

CHAPTER ONE

By any measure of such things, Martha Pootes was an uncommonly attractive young woman. At the tender age of eighteen she was tall and clean-limbed, and even wearing a plain, high-necked dress, there was no disguising the enviable feminine curves that lay beneath the rough material. Flawless skin, good teeth and flowing strawberry blonde hair all contributed to the allusion of perfection ... or something very close to it. Her glorious attributes were all the more remarkable considering that she and her parents lived an often hard, physical life in that south-western corner of Kentucky.

The Pootes' farm was situated near the town of LaFayette in aptly named Christian County. A God-fearing family, they grew, amongst other things, corn, Irish potatoes, apples and cabbages, and all without the use of slave labour because, unlike some of their neighbours, her pa didn't hold with the 'peculiar institution'. And even though it was January of that year, 1862, all the paid field hands were engaged at some task or other, well away from the simple, single-storeyed timber house that was the family home. By a strange twist of fate her parents, having put off the trip for some time, had taken their only wagon into the small settlement to purchase some much needed necessities, with the avowed intention of returning before darkness fell. All of which meant that, for the time being at least, their daughter was entirely alone.

As an only child, temporary solitude held no fears for Martha. She knew all the residents of the farms surrounding her, and the War of Secession hadn't yet touched that part of the Union. In fact, seeing as most of the belligerents were back east, it was entirely possible that it never would. So the only thing on her mind was the successful completion of her chores, which currently included the tub washing and mangling of various clothes. And since it was an unseasonably warm day, carrying out these tasks in the open was no hardship. So it was that she got her first look at the three strangers approaching on foot.

Had she possessed the wit to ponder such matters, Miss Pootes might have considered it strange that, although the slouching trio all wore Union blue, they were coming from the direction of the Tennessee border. That state was nominally in Confederate hands, and no one from the north had yet attempted to challenge the fact. Unbeknownst to her, all that was soon to change . . . amongst other things!

The three enlisted men tugged restlessly at their ill-fitting uniforms as they plodded along. Having become somewhat unenthusiastic volunteers in the Army of the Tennessee (River), what with all the drill and fatigues and such, they had grown tired of camp life and had decided to sneak off for a little look-see at their new surroundings. They didn't consider themselves to be deserters. From their biased viewpoint they were merely foraging for supplies, and fully intended to return to duty. . . in their own good time.

'I tell you, these poxy duds were made for a whole other body,' Brin Taylor complained, for maybe the fourth time that morning.

'Bitch, bitch, bitch. That's all you've done since the sun came up,' retorted Rab Forrest, although in truth he would happily have thrown his own uniform into the nearest ditch, and not just because it didn't fit properly. The enlistment bounties they had all received had long since been spent, and he was beginning to find army life, with its ever-present bawling non-coms, altogether far too demanding.

'Mayhap we should turn our hands to farming,' Jason Metford contributed in a far more considered tone. 'Because if the locals all look like *her*, we couldn't go far wrong.' It was the tone, as much as the content of what he said, that immediately took his companions' attention.

Grinding to a halt on the dusty lane, the trio of Union soldiers stared towards the farmhouse and its outbuildings. As though by divine timing, the winter sun suddenly highlighted the young woman standing by the iron mangle.

'By Christ, she's a real peach,' Forrest muttered hungrily.

'Do that mean we're in Georgia?' Taylor queried with what *might* have been a weak attempt at humour.

'It means we're in heaven, you moron,' Metford retorted. 'Leastways we will be if we play our cards right . . . or even if we don't.' With that ominous comment, he straightened his back and shifted the Springfield rifle musket on his shoulder, so as to appear more like the soldier that he was supposed to be. His lean features suddenly sported a hungry expression that had nothing to do with the need for food. 'Shape up, you scruffy sons of bitches. Let's give the little lady something to be proud of. After all, she's what we're fighting for, or maybe over. Haw, haw, haw.'

Martha had no experience of soldiery, from any man's army, so at the first sight of these mysterious newcomers she felt a thrill of childlike anticipation. Like everyone else, she had heard the rumours that a host of Mister Lincoln's 'boys' was gathered around Cairo, in the adjacent state of Illinois, but she had never expected to actually encounter any of them. And yet, as they tramped closer down the rutted track, excitement gradually turned to apprehension. They carried rifles, for sure, but there was nothing fresh-faced or good-looking about any of these young warriors underneath their thoroughly impractical forage caps. In fact one of them looked more like a Mississippi River pirate from one of the tales her pa

10

used to tell, back when she had been a youngster. This impression was emphasized by a large black mark seared into the flesh under his right eye, as though an eye patch had slipped from its rightful place.

Then one of the others leered at her and called out, 'Howdy do, young missy?' and she felt a sudden urge to race into the house and bar the door. Yet her own sense of decency prevented her from doing that, because what if they merely wanted directions or a drink of water? And by the time she had agonized over that, it was too late. They were in the yard, surveying the buildings.

'Spread like this bespeaks of a lot of folks,' Metford observed, as he gratefully slipped the long gun from his shoulder and placed the butt proprietorially on the ground. Then, gently rubbing the powder burn, his dissolute eyes settled on the young woman and began to peruse every inch of her body.

Forrest, who possessed little original thought but was quick on the uptake, followed on with, 'Yeah, where is everyone? We was hoping for a parley. Ain't never been in these parts before.'

Martha, who hadn't been raised to lie, answered instinctively: 'The hired hands are out in the fields. My ma and pa have gone over to the general store in LaFayette.' The words had barely passed her lips before she realized her mistake and quickly added, 'But they'll all be back mighty soon.'

Metford favoured her with a fleeting smile that somehow only emphasized his unpleasant demeanour. Suggestively licking his lips, he drawled, 'Is that a fact? Guess we'd better take our pleasures while we can, then.' With that, he reached out and ran a grubby forefinger down her left cheek. An unpleasant aroma of stale sweat and whiskey emanated from him.

Martha stepped back sharply. Real fear abruptly coursed through her body. 'Don't you do that again, mister!' she snapped. 'I've got a shotgun inside!'

Metford's eyes widened in simulated fright. With elaborate ceremony he leaned his Springfield against the suddenly redundant mangle, and then without any warning let loose a stinging open-handed slap across her face. The blow was completely unexpected, and sent her reeling back towards the house. 'Guess you should have thought of that sooner,' he mocked.

Forrest crowded up behind him, keen to join in the fun. 'Hee, hee,' was all he could manage.

Only Taylor seemed uncomfortable with the dark turn of events. 'This don't seem right to me, Jase,' he protested. 'She's barely more than a child.'

Metford didn't take his eyes from Martha as he retorted. 'She's more than woman enough for me. If your pecker ain't up for it, stay the hell out here an' keep watch instead.' So saying, he hooked his fingers inside the collar of her dress and heaved down on the material. The outer garment tore clean in two, revealing a plain shift beneath, which now strained against the sudden press of her breasts as she drew in a great breath to scream. Moving rapidly, he grabbed the terrified girl by the throat, choking off the cry, and then thrust her across the threshold into the parlour.

Accustomed to hard physical work, Martha kicked and struggled violently, but it was all to no avail against the overwhelming strength of the lustful soldier. Conscious of Forrest following him into the parlour, Metford abruptly slammed a clenched fist into his victim's stomach, then pushed her down on to the dirt floor. Retching against the awful pain and nausea emanating from her belly, Martha's brief resistance was entirely over.

'I get first pickings,' he barked back at his excited companion, before yanking up the flimsy clothing to reveal Martha's shapely legs.

'Well, sure, Jase. Watching ain't no hardship to me,' Forrest replied, almost drooling at the sight of her bare flesh. And so, in a casual encounter that was fated to have terrible consequences, the brutal assault on Martha Pootes began.

Throughout her dreadful ordeal, Brin Taylor remained outside, nervously watching the surrounding fields. Periodically, muffled screams came from within the house, and at one point a creaking door over at the barn had him reaching for the hammer on his Springfield.

'You fellas nearly done?' he called out hopefully, but that was greeted by raucous laughter and yet another agonized wail from their victim. 'This is just plain wrong,' he muttered unhappily. His scalp began to get sticky with sweat, and so he carelessly tugged the forage cap from his head. All his instincts cried out for him to clear off and leave them to it, but for some reason he remained rooted to the spot. And although slow-witted, deep down he knew why: he had a fear of being alone, because for much of his short life he had been. And unlike most folks, his two companions at least tolerated him and didn't mock him . . . too much.

Two things then occurred almost simultaneously. Taylor caught sight of distant movement out in the fields, and Metford staggered out of the house. The rapist's face was coated in sweat, and a dreamy look filled his eyes. More shockingly, his grubby hands were now spattered with blood. The reluctant lookout shook his head in horrified dismay. What had they done to the poor girl? Then he recalled his sighting and pointed off across the farmland.

'There's people moving over yonder, and I reckon they're heading this way.'

In truth, Taylor had no idea who was heading where, but thankfully his disclosure had a sobering effect on Metford. That man's eyes widened momentarily, and then he stumbled over to the nearby water trough. Plunging his head deep into it, he stayed under for long moments. When he finally came up for air, his sharp wits had fully returned.

'Leave that bitch to her misery!' he hollered back into the house, as he washed his hands clean of blood. 'You hear me, Rab? You've had your turn, an' then some. There's folks on the move out here, and we don't want to have to pay for our pleasures . . . in any way at all.'

After much cursing, Forrest finally appeared on the threshold. He, too, was sweating and blood-stained, and unhappy at being interrupted. 'Aw shit, Jase. I was just getting started . . . again.' But then, as the stark realities of what they had done began to register with him, he surveyed his surroundings with guilty apprehension. 'What folks? Where?' he demanded. 'I don't see no . . . .'

Metford cut him short. 'Get yourself cleaned up, pronto. We're moving out.'

Thoroughly spooked by the state of his cronies, that was music to Taylor's ears. Yet it did pose a question. 'Where to?'

'Back to the Army of the Tennessee, of course.'

Taylor was aghast. 'After all this? What if someone comes looking for you . . . *us*?'

Metford, rearranging his clothing, regarded him pityingly. 'You see these uniforms? Well, where we're going, there's thousands more of them. What chance has anyone got of picking us out? And that little bitch sure won't be travelling anywhere for a long time.' The thought of what he had just done brought a smile of pleasure to his face. 'Hot dang, but we sure showed her a good time!'

As Forrest headed over to the water trough, Taylor, against his better judgement, tentatively approached the door to the house. Although not having partici-pated in the savage rape, he was nevertheless afflicted by a morbid curiosity to view its results. What he saw brought hot bile up into his throat. How could his *friends* have done such as this to an innocent young girl? Every stitch of clothing had been removed, and blood glistened across parts of her prostrate and abused body. For a shocking moment, he actually thought she was dead, until a low moan passed her lips. Recoiling in horror, he turned to find the others grinning at him.

'If this is what war's like, I'm all for it,' proclaimed Metford cheerily. With that, he hoisted the Springfield over his shoulder and headed off towards the southwest without a backward glance. Forrest and Taylor had no choice other than to follow him, because both of them in their own way looked to the powder-marked brigand for leadership. It was not until the site of their dreadful deeds was lost from view that Brin Taylor abruptly realized that he was no longer wearing his army issue forage cap.

'Well, no matter,' he decided. He would just have to make do without, because there was no way in hell that he was going back for it.

As for Martha Pootes, she was finally left alone with her misery to await discovery by whosoever was unfortunate enough to return to the farmhouse first. The question was, would she even survive long enough to see them?

CHAPTER TWO

As promised, Brett and Jenny Pootes returned to the farm well before sunset. In addition to the essential purchases in the back of the wagon, they had picked out a new dress for their treasured only child. Gaily coloured but modest, it would be ideal for Sunday best when attending LaFayette's recently constructed Methodist Church. As they rattled into sight of the buildings, they had no inkling that their settled lives were about to be irrevocably changed ... for the worse. The first indication of trouble came as Brett reined in the team near the barn and glanced over at the two white-faced field hands waiting in front of the house.

'What ails thee, Jacob?' he called out to the nearest. 'Looks like you done seen a ghost.'

That man shook his head in dismay as he moved towards them. 'There ain't no easy way to state this, boss. So I'll just up and say it. Martha's been kilt!'

Brett's jaw silently dropped in disbelief, but his wife was far more vocal. After uttering a piercing scream, she leapt from the wagon and raced for the house, all the while calling out her daughter's name. Coming to his senses, her husband wasn't far behind. What they discovered was the stuff of nightmares, and it was some minutes before Brett could speak with any rationality. Finally, he turned to Jacob, who had tentatively followed them in.

'In God's name, what happened to her?' he demanded.

The field hand blew out his cheeks like a horse. 'This is how we found her, Mister Pootes. Thought it best to let her stay where she lay. The bastards what did this must have hurt her real bad, 'cause she didn't last long.'

With his wife continuing to mutter incoherently over their deceased and still naked daughter, Brett's eyes widened like saucers. 'Who *were* they? *Where* are they?'

Jacob, normally a solid, taciturn character, began wringing his large hands in obvious distress. Like all the other employees, he had been captivated by Martha's delightful beauty and innocence. Her death was undoubtedly the most unpleasant thing he had ever witnessed.

'None of us caught sight of anyone, boss. But Martha, well . . . she managed a few words before she passed. Apparently there were three of them, an' they all wore Union blue.'

'Soldiers!' Brett exclaimed. 'Which way did they go?'

Jacob shrugged unhappily. 'She didn't say. An'

18

seeing as this is where we found her, it's likely she never saw them again after they left the house. Happen there's a couple of things that might help, though. Seems how the leader had a powder burn under his right eye. And I found this on the floor, near to her . . . body.' So saying, he tugged a screwed-up forage cap from his pocket and handed it over.

Brett stared at it for a long moment before clambering to his feet and heading for the door. The stomach-churning sight of Martha, coated in dried blood and gone forever, coupled with Jenny's now constant moaning, had suddenly got too much for him. He needed some space. Bursting across the threshold, and oblivious to the shocked stare of the other field hand, he raced back on to the lane. There he peered wildly about him, as though willing the marauders to reappear. Of course they were long gone, and after a while that fact dawned on him. But one thing was undeniable. They were out there somewhere, and come what may, they were going to pay for what they had done to his daughter!

It wasn't until the following day that the grieving parents were able to discuss rationally what should be done next. Martha's broken body had been meticulously cleaned and clothed, and now lay on a table in one corner of the parlour. Jacob had been dispatched to Lafayette to fetch a preacher. Brett was in the feverish process of constructing a coffin from some rough-cut timber left over from constructing the barn, on account of the fact that the town wasn't big enough to support an undertaker. But although he knuckled down to the task well enough, it was obvious that his heart was filled with hatred and his mind set on revenge.

'As soon as Martha has been decently buried, I aim to seek out those murdering bastards.' His eyes seemed to burn as he spoke, and there could be no doubting his determination. Yet Jenny's response was not at all what he might have expected.

'That's a mighty foolish notion, husband. You don't know where to look, or how to go about it. Anything could happen to you. You could even end up conscripted into the army, for God's sake! And what about the farm . . . and me? There could be more of that scum out there. These ain't normal times.'

Brett was taken aback, and paused in his work to stare at his wife. Her words had shocked him, and all the more so because she was probably right. Anything he attempted would be like shooting in the dark. And could he really go off and leave her when there might indeed be more scavengers in the area? Although nearing forty and showing signs of a hard life, Jenny Pootes was still a very handsome woman.

'But I can't just do nothing,' he exclaimed, suddenly feeling strangely helpless.

She sighed and then locked her sad eyes on his. 'Getting these men could well be a hard and unpleasant task. Which means it will need a hard and unpleasant man to take it on.' She abruptly ceased talking and waited for his reaction. It wasn't long in coming.

'Frank!'

'The very same.'

Brett shook his head doubtfully. 'It must be ten years since we clapped eyes on him. With his line of work, he might even be dead. An' besides, since when did you consider him unpleasant?'

Jenny chose to ignore the deeper meaning, and shook her head emphatically. 'Your brother ain't the dying kind. But there's one way to find out. Contact him.'

'How?' Brett queried, although deep down he knew exactly how.

His wife, understanding his reluctance, decided to humour him. 'You get back into town and send a telegraph message to the marshal's office in Frankfort. If he is still drawing breath, they'll likely know where to find him.'

Brett still wasn't convinced. 'Even if they do, he might not come.'

Jenny, her nerves already shot to hell, abruptly lost patience. 'For Christ's sake! If you say what's happened to Martha, he'll come, for sure. You know he will. Just do it!'

And so it was decided. Brett would briefly return to LaFayette to send his message, while Jenny, shotgun in hand, kept the field hands near the house. And God help anyone who attempted to molest her!

It was exactly one week later when a lone horseman reined in a few hundred yards from the prosperous-looking spread. Deputy United States Marshal Frank

Pootes surveyed the farm with mixed feelings. The last time he and his brother had met, some very harsh words had passed between them. And in the years since their final parting, Frank had been tormented by a great many regrets, made all the worse because he had been mostly to blame for the rift. Consequently, he had genuinely believed that they would never see each other again. But then he received the ghastly telegraph message about little Martha, and that changed everything.

Sighing, the marshal urged his mount over towards the buildings. Reaching easy pistol range, he very deliberately called out, 'Hello the house!' He well knew that after such a dark turn of events, the grieving occupants might be more than a little trigger-happy. His need for caution was confirmed when the gaping muzzles of a shotgun appeared in the doorway. 'I ain't no threat to law-abiding citizens, so don't you go popping any caps on me,' he added.

The door opened wide, and suddenly there was his brother. 'Landsakes!' Brett exclaimed. 'It's really you.' He quickly lowered the twelve-gauge, and then stood rather awkwardly gazing at his sibling. It occurred to him that Frank looked a good deal older. There were grey flecks in his dark hair, and the lines in his strong, handsome face were more pronounced. But then, of course, a decade was an awful long time, and none of them were immune from its ravages.

'Well, I guess that under the circumstances, you're gonna be inviting me in,' Frank remarked as he slowly dismounted. 'So I'll just let this old horse have a drink out of your trough.'

Brett was abruptly shoved forward beyond the threshold, so that his wife was able to join them. 'Hello Frank,' she said softly, her cheeks strangely tinged with colour. 'I . . . that is *we* wondered if you were still alive.'

'Well, now you know,' Frank retorted, rather more sharply than he had intended. Then, suddenly anxious to match her softer tone, he continued with, 'You're looking well, Missus Pootes. The years have been kind to you . . . unlike this ornery husband of yourn.'

Brett grunted. After such a long separation he was sorely tempted to continue with the banter for a while, but then his eyes flicked to the freshly dug grave, and instead all he said was, 'You'd best come in, brother. We've got things to discuss, an' none of it good.'

The lawman followed his line of sight and stiffened. 'So that fool telegraph operator didn't get it wrong then,' he commented grimly. Shaking his head sadly, he tethered his horse and then strode slowly over to join them. 'I reckon you'd better tell me all about it.'

The cost per word of sending a telegram meant that the message to the marshal's office in Frankfort had been necessarily brief. Only once he had heard the full, shocking tale did Frank Pootes realize what he was up against. And yet he had no hesitation in agreeing to seek justice on their behalf. After all, apart from the fact that kin were involved, it was his job. Unfortunately, it was far from being a straight-forward task of finding and apprehending fugitives, a fact that both Brett and Jenny seemed to comprehend.

'If they've returned to the Union army, what can you do?' queried Jenny anxiously. 'After all, you've only got the slimmest of descriptions, and there must be more than one man in all those thousands with a powder burn on his face.'

Frank got up from his chair in the parlour. He was a big man, six feet tall or more, and not used to enclosed spaces. After a moment or two he began to prowl around. There was far more to all this than just identifying the suspects, and somehow movement helped him get his thoughts together. 'If Martha, a citizen of these United States, was kilt by a Union soldier, then that makes it a *federal* offence. And I'm a *federal* law officer, which gives me some jurisdiction. Although I gotta say, a lot depends on how coopera-tive the commanding officer chooses to be. On his own ground, a general in charge of an army is akin to a god. As for finding them, well, I'm kind of hoping they'll find me, once word gets around that I'm hunting them. Which, one way or another, it will do!'

Brett nodded his understanding. Despite his awful loss, there was now at least a spark of hope in his eyes. 'So you intend to ride over to Cairo then?'

'Cairo?' Frank retorted. 'I'd say not! Last I heard

there's a general, name of Grant, moving his forces down into Tennessee. Seems like he aims to have a crack at the rebels. And if you ask me, it's about damn time someone did.'

Brett absorbed all that before mentioning something that still prayed on his mind. 'What you propose sounds mighty dangerous. So by rights I should be going with you. You could deputise me, or whatever it is you'd need to do.'

'No!' His brother's response couldn't have been more emphatic. 'There could be more of those cockchafers on the loose. Americans fighting Americans just ain't natural, and it's unleashed all kinds of unpleasantness. So you ain't going anywhere if it means leaving this lovely wife of yourn on her lonesome. And don't say that you've got hired hands to protect her, 'cause they'll likely just cut and run at the first whiff of gunsmoke.'

'Some of that's kind of similar to what she said,' Brett ruefully acknowledged.

'Which just goes to prove she's the brains of the family,' Frank retorted.

'When do you intend to go after them?' Jenny's question was unintentionally prickly, and she quickly tried to soften it with a sad smile. 'Not that we're anxious to be rid of you after all this time, Frank. Only. . . .'

The marshal returned the smile. 'After what's occurred here, you don't have to explain to me, Jen.'

Brett glanced sharply at his brother. He never shortened his wife's name, and so it had been an awful long time since he had heard her called that. Inevitably it drew his thoughts back to the time when Frank had overstepped the boundaries that should exist between a brother and his wife. As all of them were suddenly enveloped by a variety of memories, an uncomfortable silence descended over the room. It was the lawman that finally broke it.

'Little Martha,' he said hesitantly. 'Did she grow up to be a beautiful young woman?'

Tears welled up in Jenny's eyes as she nodded. 'Lovely looks and a lovely nature.' For a brief moment her face was serene, before it suddenly twisted into an ugly, bitter mask of hatred. 'You get those bastards for me, Frank. You hear? Every last one of them!'

That man sighed. As a peace officer he had sworn on a bible to administer justice, not vengeance. Then again, these were not normal times. His country was at war with itself. And his niece had just been brutally murdered. Perhaps it was time to take the Old Testament literally. An eye for an eye, and a tooth for a tooth!

CHAPTER THREE

The following morning saw Frank Pootes continue his journey in a south-westerly direction. In truth he was glad to be back in the saddle again. Despite, or maybe because of the fact that he hadn't seen Brett and his wife for a decade, it had been a strained parting, with a lot of things left unsaid. And yet he had only himself to blame for the long separation. Or had he? After all, 'Jen' had been more than willing, all those years before.

'God damn it all to hell!' he exclaimed to the empty country around him. There was little to be gained from chewing over past mistakes. Best to concentrate on making amends. That alone was shaping up to be one heck of a challenge.

As horse and rider jogged along, Pootes extracted the relatively new forage cap from his jacket pocket and stared at it contemplatively. Not surprisingly it had no personalized identification marks of any kind. It was just one of thousands upon thousands that had been issued during the last year. In his

27

opinion, after such an occurrence in nominally friendly territory, it was likely that the three scavengers had returned to their regiment to lie low. There was safety in numbers, even if it did mean rejoining the war.

In addition to his being a *federal* law officer, Marshal Pootes had one more ace that he could play. Although officially part of the Union, Kentucky was a border state. Many of its people had leanings towards the south, and many held slaves of their own. Consequently, President Lincoln intended to do everything possible not to upset the state's inhabitants, and risk them changing allegiance. Rape and murder of its citizens by his soldiery didn't fit any definition of treading lightly, and could just give the marshal an edge when dealing with the army's commander.

Tucking the peeked cap away, the lawman urged his horse to greater speed. He didn't know exactly where he was headed, but one thing was for sure: an army of some fifteen thousand men couldn't be that hard to locate. The only down side was that he might run into Confederate forces by mistake. That would make his task difficult indeed!

It was late the following afternoon when Frank Pootes first caught sight of the Union forces. Much earlier that day he had forded the Cumberland River, and not long after had decided that he was probably in the State of Tennessee. A well-honed instinct for trouble then told him that somewhere up ahead there would be a great mass of men . . . and sure enough he had found them. Of course all that had been the easy bit, because approaching an army in the field could be mighty risky, especially as the winter sun was heading for the horizon. Poorly trained and jumpy pickets were likely to be trigger happy.

For long moments, Pootes pondered whether to stay clear and wait for morning, but finally decided against it. Being so close he couldn't risk a fire, and yet he had little desire to spend the night in a cold camp. Although the days had recently been very pleasant, it was still the middle of winter and the nights could be gruelling.

Mind made up, he urged his horse over towards a stand of trees, from where smoke curled lazily upwards, and the delicious smell of frying bacon was accompanied by muted chatter. It seemed to make far more sense to head directly for the pickets and announce his presence, rather than attempt to sneak past and get shot from the flank. At some twenty yards distance, and still apparently undiscovered, the lawman reined in. Extending his open palms outwards, as though in supplication, he took a deep breath and called out.

'Hello the fire. Don't go popping any caps on me, you hear? I ain't no southern scarecrow.'

His announcement was initially greeted by startled silence, but then a voice barked out, 'You got him, Baker?'

From somewhere off to Pootes' left there came the

distinctive double click as the hammer on a firearm was cocked. 'I got him.'

That disclosure was received with a chuckle, and then a blue-coated figure appeared from the trees, to be closely followed by two more. The leader sported three blue chevrons on his sleeves, and all of them carried Springfield rifle muskets with vicious-looking socket bayonets attached.

'Looks like we caught us a skulker,' the non-com remarked. 'What say we get some shackles on him before that bacon's ready?'

The others laughed, and swaggered forwards. At the sight of a mere civilian, the soldiers had assumed an air of importance out of all proportion to their rank. With a sheen of sweat forming on his brow, Pootes recognized that such dangerous talk had to be nipped in the bud, pronto.

'I ain't no skulker,' he barked. 'And any buck sergeant that tries to shackle me will end up busted back to private before the day's out!'

The non-com's eyes narrowed, and abruptly his vicious-looking bayonet point advanced on the new-comer. 'Just who the hell are you, mister?'

It was only then that the marshal, cursing at his omission, realized that he had neglected to display his badge of office. Since he didn't always wish to advertise his occupation, he kept it pinned behind the broad lapel of his jacket. Very slowly reaching up, he pulled back the material to reveal a small medieval shield with a five-pointed star at its centre. Then, patting it proprietorially, he announced:

'Deputy United States Marshal Frank Pootes. I'm here to see your general.'

The sergeant blinked with astonishment, but wasn't yet quite ready to buckle. 'You'll need to do better than that,' he retorted. 'We got lots of generals.'

Pootes sighed in a display of obvious impatience. 'General Grant, of course. I want the organ grinder, not the monkeys!'

That produced a few sniggers, and then after pointedly staring off to his left, the marshal thankfully heard the hammer being lowered on the hidden sharpshooter's long gun.

'Guess we'd better let you through, then,' the sergeant finally and very reluctantly allowed. 'At least as far as the captain, anyhu. Elijah, you go on and escort this law dog into camp.'

The designated private was unimpressed with his assignment. 'The hell you say! What about my bacon, Sarge?'

'Well, if you're lucky we might just save your bacon,' that man retorted with a brief chuckle, as he turned away towards the enticing cooking fire. Then, as the others hooted with amuscment, he suddenly realized that he'd actually uttered a pretty passable jest, and so added, 'But don't count on it, soldier!'

Pootes dismounted and followed the disgruntled soldier through the screen of trees. 'Seems like rank always has its privileges, don't it?' the lawman commented, with just a hint of sarcasm.

'Say what?' Elijah queried dumbly, as he screwed

31

up his grimy features. From the look of his blackened teeth, chewing on any meat would present quite a challenge.

And then, all of a sudden, they found themselves in the open, and Pootes blinked with a mixture of shock and awe. In all his years he couldn't recall having seen so much humanity in one place. Vast numbers of large, conical Sibley tents, big enough to accommodate a whole squad and ranged in company streets, dotted the meadows stretching down to the Tennessee River. By one of the many quirks of fate that influenced this internecine conflict, they had actually been developed by a career West Pointer who was now a serving general with the Confederacy.

In front of each canvas shelter there was a cooking fire that would likely never be extinguished. Enterprising sutlers had set up shop around the massive encampment, selling pies, gingerbreads and candy. Such abundance would have been the envy of the South, as it was very likely that the armies of the Union were the best equipped of any nation in history. And as if all of this wasn't intimidating enough, moored on the river was a squadron of seven steam-powered gunboats. Even the rapidly expanding US Navy had got in on the act!

'Quite a turnout,' Pootes commented thoughtfully. Since it was highly likely that Martha's killers were somewhere in this vast horde, and it was down to him alone to find them, it was only now that he fully appreciated just what he was up against.

*

Brigadier General Ulysses S. Grant was a stubby, unprepossessing fellow, who nevertheless held one's attention, and not just because of the single silver star resplendent in the epaulette on each shoulder of his rumpled blue uniform. It was the eyes. There was something about them that suggested great wisdom . . . or at the very least the ability to somehow control other men and influence events. And unlike many other high-ranking officers, he was also surprisingly accessible. Once Pootes had finally reached the captain in charge of the pickets, it had then been far easier to obtain an audience with the commander of the Army of the Tennessee than to get through his lines. The general stood next to his campaign cot, one hand grasping the central support post of the large tent, as he closely scrutinized the newcomer.

'So what brings you to this neck of the woods, Marshal?' Grant enquired, straight to the point but courteously enough. Since he was chewing on a cigar at the time, his words had been mumbled, but his eyes had already taken in Pootes' badge of office, and the very recently developed rifle in his grasp.

The lawman was equally direct. 'Seems like three of your men done raped and murdered a young woman near LaFayette, Kentucky, some nine days ago. She survived long enough to describe their appearance. They all wore Union blue.' Producing the forage cap, he added, 'And this here's my *bona fides.*'

There had been something very intense about the lawman's delivery, which prompted Grant to frown.

'She kin of yours?'

'My niece!'

The soldier bit deeply into his cigar butt. 'Damn it all to hell!' he exclaimed through gritted teeth. For long moments he stared at the ground, scratching his close-cropped beard, before abruptly transferring all his attention to his visitor. 'My sincere condolences, Marshal, but what gives you the right to pursue them into the midst of an army at war? My army. And to trouble me with such matters? I have numerous things to think on. Only tomorrow my forces advance against the rebels holding Fort Henry. It is quite possible that many men will die . . . including the ones you seek.'

Pootes nodded, but held his ground. 'I'll allow you've one hell of a job to do, General, but I, too, am a federal officer and I'm trying to do mine. I claim jurisdiction because Martha Pootes was a citizen of the United States, killed by federal employees. An' I'm sure you know how President Lincoln wants Union forces to stay on good terms with the folks up in Kentucky.' He paused for effect for a moment, before summing up: 'These sons of bitches need trying and hanging. An' that's the reason why I'm here.'

There was relative quiet in the tent for a while as Grant pondered the matter, allowing sounds of camp life to intrude. Then the General struck a Lucifer to ignite an oil lamp against the encroaching darkness. Only when that was lit to his satisfaction did he answer. 'You state your case well, Marshal.'

Sensing there was more to come, Pootes remained silent and merely nodded his acknowledgement.

'You have my permission to remain with this army and search for these varmints. But if you should get caught up in any fighting, don't come crying to me. There'll be killing a plenty on the morrow. My aide, Captain Bragg, will see that you are allocated a tent, and will do anything else to assist you that doesn't affect his normal duties.'

The lawman was pleasantly surprised, but he hadn't quite finished: 'Might I trouble you for one more consideration, General?'

Grant raised his dark eyebrows, but presented no objection.

'It occurs to me that the quickest way to locate these pus weasels is to put the word out that I'm here and hunting them.'

The soldier's eyes widened expressively, before he chuckled his appreciation. 'Ain't that a mite dangerous?'

Pootes shrugged, and hefted the very impressive Henry rifle in his left hand. 'A marshal's life can indeed be hard and short, but I didn't come down with yesterday's rain. I'll be ready for them!'

'Well then, I will do as you ask, and I wish you luck,' General Grant retorted, before moving over to sit behind his portable desk. The interview was obviously over, yet as Pootes turned to leave, the soldier did offer one parting but rather obscure comment: 'And I would advise you to keep clear of the pickets at dawn.'

It was the distinctive crackle of musketry that woke Pootes from a deep slumber. A sharp chill of fear momentarily enveloped him, until he suddenly recalled General Grant's parting words. With that recollection came the realization that after a cold, damp night, the pickets were clearing their rifles prior to loading with fresh powder. Such a procedure would provide an ideal opportunity to take a shot at any unwelcome visitor foolish enough to get within range. . . from any direction. And since the Springfield could be deadly up to one thousand yards, this knowledge provided little comfort.

For long moments the marshal lay on his bedroll in the small tent assigned to him. Pondering the sanity of deliberately advertising both his presence and his objective, he briefly considered asking for the decision to be reversed. Then, as the fog of sleep departed, he cursed himself for a lame-brained fool. The commanding general had given every impression of being capable and efficient. Word of the lawman's mission had doubtless already been circulated, so any regrets were pointless. Far better to consider his next step.

Increasing noise and activity around him finally persuaded him to make a move. Clambering to his feet, he cautiously pulled back the tent flap and peered out. As on his arrival, the scene before him took his breath away. There were so many uniformed men in sight that it was like viewing an ant colony from its centre. Yet unlike the previous day, the army was now obviously preparing for departure. Non-commissioned officers were bellowing orders, and tents were being dismantled and loaded on to wagons. And over on the river, the gunboats were building up a head of steam.

As he stepped out into the open, Pootes abruptly became the centre of interest to those soldiers immediately closest. It had been dark when he had taken possession of his tent, but now he was in full view of everyone. To his experienced eye, their reactions were revealing, because they proved beyond doubt that all the men now knew him for what he was. Some looked at the ground, others abruptly found the sky of great interest, whilst the bolder ones stared at him with blatant dislike. None of them offered any form of greeting. Such was the life of a lawman. When someone needed the law enforcing, he was suddenly their best friend; but the rest of the time it was as though he were a leper. It had always been that way. Well used to all this, the only thing of relevance to Marshal Pootes was that none of them filled Martha's sparse description.

'Back to work, you men,' came a commanding voice, and abruptly all was hustle and bustle again.

Captain Bragg, whom Pootes had met the night before, appeared at his side. 'They're mostly simple folk, with no love for lawmen,' he remarked. 'But I figure that'll be nothing new for you.'

'Ain't that the truth?' the marshal drawled as he scrutinized the officer.

37

Bragg appeared to be about thirty years old. Tall and unfashionably clean-shaven, he gave every appearance of competence, which, serving as an aide to General Grant, was probably a necessary requirement. His uniform was well brushed, and his captain's bars gleamed in the morning light. And he wasn't just paying a social call. His speech was brisk and to the point.

'As you can see, sir, the army is fixing to move against the enemy. And there is a deal of urgency, because we don't want the damn navy getting there first and stealing the glory. At some point there will undoubtedly be a deal of violence, so if you are determined to accompany us, it would behove you to remain at the rear . . . for your own safety.'

Having said his piece, the harassed officer made to leave, but Pootes also intended to have his say. 'Don't you trouble yourself about my safety, Captain. Violence and I are old acquaintances. But there are certain things I would know.'

Bragg chewed his bottom lip before nodding agreement. It was obvious that although extremely preoccupied, he was under orders to cooperate.

'The men that I am hunting must have left the army for some days. They probably only returned to lie low in case of any pursuit. Would their absence have been noted, because that could help me?'

The captain shook his head. 'Grant has been receiving a great many reinforcements. On top of that, his army has been on the move for some time.' He paused as though slightly embarrassed. 'There is a great deal of administration to catch up on. Three men would have had no difficulty dropping out of the line on some pretext.'

Pootes grunted. 'OK then, so how about this? I believe that these varmints are fighting soldiers, not part of the supply chain. And if so, then I will have to go where they are. Who commands at the front?'

Bragg raised his eyebrows in surprise, before apparently smiling at some private joke. 'General Smith is ordered to advance on Fort Henry with elements of the 11th Indiana and the 18th Illinois amongst others. If you run up against him, he's sure to make an impression on you.'

Pootes wasn't too sure what to make of that, but chose to ignore it. 'Well then, that is where I must go.'

The captain shrugged. 'Be it on your own head, Marshal, though I sure do wonder how you intend to find three fugitives amongst all those men – but I guess you know your business. Good luck to you.' And with that he turned away to go about his business.

It was Pootes' turn to smile. He had deliberately withheld the detail regarding the powder burn, in case it should spread and prompt the culprit to desert. So now, all he had to do was keep searching until he found a soldier with a black mark under his eye. Simple, really!

'You see the son of a bitch, Rab?'
   'Oh yeah!'

'Well, if *we* can, then so will the Johnny Rebs once we close in. Especially if he's sashaying about on his high horse. An' anything could happen near that fort, what with all the shooting an' all. So if they don't get him, we surely will.'

'That don't seem right, Jase,' Taylor whined. 'Killing a marshal's a sure way to trouble. Besides, I took no part in those bad deeds at the farm, an' I don't want any part of this.'

'Shut your mouth, Brin, or you'll go the way of the law dog!' Metford snarled. 'You was there when it happened, an' that's all that counts. Besides, I wasn't to know we'd kilt the bitch. But look at it this way, at least she died happy! Haw, haw!'

CHAPTER FOUR

Brigadier General Charles Ferguson Smith was a
career soldier and disciplinarian of the old school. A
one time Commandant of Cadets at West Point, he
had been tasked by his former pupil, Ulysses Grant,
to lead the attack on Fort Henry located in Stewart
County, Tennessee. Wise to the ways of war, he had
that morning deliberately put on a freshly laundered
white shirt under his uniform; that way, if any enemy
lead should puncture his body along with pieces of
clothing material, at least some of that would be
clean. Such a precaution indicated that he expected
the assault to be a bloody business.

Not known for his patience, Smith was currently
incensed at the very real prospect of the navy stealing
a march on him. The five-sided, Confederate-held
fort was situated on low swampy ground on the
eastern bank of the Tennessee River. Because of the
difficult terrain, Smith's advance was quite literally
getting bogged down, whereas the seven gunboats
were of course in their element. Already within range

on the army's right flank, their eight-inch Dahlgrens were efficiently pounding the distant walls. They weren't having it all their own way, though. The rebel stronghold also boasted a number of artillery pieces, which were scoring notable hits on the approaching flotilla.

Consequently, as his cursing troops floundered in the mire, it didn't take much to raise the general's bile. The sight of an unknown mounted civilian moving apparently haphazardly in amongst his struggling infantry was more than enough to get the job done. His face flushed with fresh anger at such impertinence.

'Who the devil are you, sir?' he bellowed out, causing his impressive white mustachios to shake, as though in a strong wind.

Marshal Pootes had a great many things on his mind, not least of which was checking every man he encountered for a distinctive mark on the face, and so he didn't immediately respond.

'Answer me, damn you, or I'll have you in irons!' the general continued, his voice increasing in power.

'Someone else out to shackle me,' Pootes muttered, before urging his mount over towards the increasingly impatient Smith. Carefully he threaded his way through the slowly advancing bluecoats, very conscious of the fierce gaze locked on to him. Only after displaying his marshal's shield did he finally reply, briefly but succinctly explaining both the reason for his presence, and on whose authority he was there.

The general stared at him askance. 'In case you hadn't realized, this country is at war with itself. Every one of these men is likely to be a killer after today. That's if we ever reach the God-damn fort. I've never seen such poor ground.'

At that moment a young officer called out from the flank. 'Shall I order the men to fix bayonets, sir?' he enquired hopefully.

Smith's features coloured even more dramatically as he angrily twisted in his saddle. 'No sir, you shall not! I can't even see the enemy yet.' Returning his attention to Pootes, he continued with, 'What you're attempting sounds like a piece of pure foolishness to me, but if you have Grant's blessing I won't hinder you. Just keep out of my damn way, is all!' With that, he spurred his mount forwards, and began urging his men to greater speed. The growing intensity of the naval bombardment was obviously working on him like a bad toothache, because it was then that he came out with an exhortation that was surely destined for the history books: 'You men volunteered to be killed for love of your country, and now you can be!'

Pootes gratefully put some distance between himself and the fractious commander, and returned to his task of inspecting grubby, sweating faces. Most of the men that he looked at simply ignored him. They knew him for what he was, and had more important matters on their minds – such as staying alive. As he shifted around in the saddle to peer under forage caps, the lawman well knew that remaining mounted made him more vulnerable. But it also gave him greater speed and an expanded field of vision. *And* he didn't have to plod through the cloying mud!

Yet as time went by and the infantry drew closer to the enemy structure, his heart began to sink. Deep down he recognized that he had taken on a hopeless task. There were just too many soldiers, and because of the increasingly chaotic advance it was getting harder to tell whose features he had checked and whose he hadn't. What he needed was for someone to panic and break cover, but then of course such a move could well cost him his life. With a sheen of sweat now coating his forehead, his search became ever more frantic. This was ridiculous. All those around him seemed to be focused on the Confederate fort, whilst he felt himself more in danger from his own side.

After what seemed like an age, the lines of muddy bluecoats got within easy rifle range of the earthen fortress. Their combative commander bellowed for them to halt. He obviously intended to take stock of the situation, and as though by divine timing at that very moment all the gunboats ceased firing, as though their commander was of the same mind. The walls of Fort Henry were clearly crumbling, but it appeared that the defenders were not yet quite ready to surrender. From the battered embrasures came a ragged volley of small arms fire.

Although no stranger to violence, Pootes looked on in horror as a number of men in the front rank jerked under impact. Some crumpled silently into the mud, whilst others screamed out in agony and shock from the dreadful wounds caused by the .58 calibre Minie balls fired by the South's British-made Enfield rifles. The lawman winced as he heard something like a bee in flight pass by his right ear. That had been far too close for comfort, but it had at least come from the direction of the enemy.

'You got him, Jase?'
  'I got him!'

The Confederates' continued resistance brought forth a shattering response from the gunboats. During the brief respite, they had moved in closer so that they were now able to fire at point blank range. The tremendous resumption of fire from the big guns was suddenly too much for Pootes' horse, which reared up in terror. Just as it did so, a neat hole was punched in its neck. With blood spurting from the wound, the doomed creature staggered back, and began to topple to one side. Clutching his rifle, the marshal pulled his boots clear of the stirrups and slipped neatly back over its haunches. By great good luck he managed to land on his feet and remain upright.

'You shot his horse, you stupid bastard!'
  'It moved sudden, is all. Caught me unawares. An' any more talk like that an' I'll shoot you next!'

*

Pootes watched in dismay as, with a great sodden thump, his faithful mount collapsed to earth, quite clearly never to rise again. Raw anger at his loss was abruptly curtailed as he realized that, because of the angle involved, the projectile could not possibly have come from Fort Henry. Moreover, if his horse hadn't reared up, it would undoubtedly have been him lying in the mire. The consequences of his dangerous ploy had definitely come home to roost. As a chill came over him, he raised his repeater and quickly turned to cover his left flank.

A crouching private glanced up at him and sneered. 'Now you're on foot like the rest of us, Mister Law Dog!'

'The enemy's that a-way, soldier,' Pootes brusquely retorted, jerking his thumb towards the besieged fort.

The grimy fellow grunted something unintelligible as Pootes brushed past him. The cloying mud meant that every step was difficult, and then the general ordered his troops to continue the advance. This meant that the marshal now had to move against the flow of cursing soldiers. And all the while he was desperately searching for a possible assassin.

'Nice gun!' a burly sergeant opined, abruptly blocking his path. The non-com's eyes were locked on the shiny brasswork of the Henry repeater. It made his cumbersome muzzle-loader look like an antique, which actually wasn't far from the truth. 'How's about a trade?'

The lawman could have supplied any number of

choice retorts, but decided to remain civil. As they stood like an island amidst the swirling sea of infantry, he replied, 'You know what I am, right?'

The sergeant nodded, but remained steadfastly in place.

'Well, my horse has just been shot dead by one of *your* men. And even now he could be aiming at the back of *your* head, just waiting for me to make a move.'

The other man's eyes widened expressively. 'Now why would some bull turd be doing a thing like that?'

A mounted officer nearby bellowed out for the sergeant to continue advancing, but he merely waved non-committedly and stayed put.

'You obviously ain't heard the *full* story. Him and two others raped my niece to death in Kentucky,' Pootes responded grimly. 'And I aim to see that they pay for their bad deeds.'

The sergeant whistled soundlessly. 'And you reckon they're back of me now, huh?'

Pootes regarded the soldier speculatively for a moment. He appeared to be hard and capable, and yet there was also an indefinable air of decency about him. The severely harassed marshal decided to take a gamble. 'They *were* when they kilt my horse,' he allowed. 'But if they've any sense at all, they'll have shifted position. There ain't much natural cover out here, so I reckon they'll keep in amongst their comrades.' He paused for a second before committing himself further. 'One thing I haven't told anyone, on account of it might could scare him into deserting, is that one of those bastards has a powder burn under his right eye.'

'You've just told me!'

Despite the circumstances, Pootes smiled broadly. 'Let's just say I'm playing a hunch, 'cause of how I maybe can't do this all on my lonesome.'

The sergeant scrutinized him intently, the possible but unlikely acquisition of a wondrous repeating rifle apparently forgotten. Then he, too, appeared to come to a decision. 'I don't hold with raping and killing womenfolk, whatever side they're on. It ain't civilized and it ain't right. What say I help you find these sons of bitches?'

Pootes eyes flickered with surprise. Assistance in the midst of a battle was the last thing that he had expected, and from a soldier at that. 'I'd be much obliged, Sergeant. . . ?'

'Rhodes. Sam Rhodes. Now enough talk. Let's move.' With that, the non-com turned on his heels. Most of the advancing infantry had passed them by, so his course took them along the rear of the men, in the general direction of where the kill shot had likely come from.

With the Union ironclads continuing to pound the fortress, the defenders had not attempted any more volleys, so it appeared that the only threat to the two men might be from their own side. Yet as they plodded on across the open ground, guns at the ready, none of the inevitable stragglers seemed to be taking any lethal interest in them.

'Seems like I was right. Whoever we're after must

have stayed with their unit,' Pootes called out. 'It'd make sense.'

'So let's join the war again and find out.' So saying, Rhodes abruptly turned to his right. As though on the scent of prey, he speeded up. Together, they ploughed through the mud and rejoined the massed ranks. Once back amongst the invasion force, because in reality that was what it was, Pootes tucked in behind the sergeant as that man pushed through the crush. His uniform and distinctive blue chevrons guaranteed easier progress, and far less resentment.

By outpacing the plodding infantry, the two men were able to weave in and out, checking facial features from left to right. Then once more the naval guns ceased firing, only this time permanently. A great cheer suddenly broke out in the ranks, as the Confederate flag was finally lowered over the severely mauled fort. But not everyone was happy about the relatively bloodless victory, because to add insult to injury the Confederate commander, Brigadier General Tilghman, had just been observed being rowed out to the Union flagship under a makeshift white flag to offer his surrender.

'God damn it all to hell,' Smith very audibly exploded from down the line. 'Those mariners will never let me forget this!'

'If he gets much closer, you'll be able to stick him with your bayonet!'

'Shut your damn mouth. I can't get a clear shot.'

*

As Rhodes ground to an abrupt halt, the hairs went up on the back of his neck. He had just spotted a powder-burnt visage. 'You see him?' he hissed.

'I see him,' Pootes replied. 'You take his rifle. I'll cover.' It made sense, because the suspect was far less likely to resist a uniformed sergeant.

Their quarry was in amongst a line of men, but because of the sudden and very unexpected victory they were milling around in joyous disorder, which made it easier for the two manhunters to approach. Sam Rhodes came up behind him, and jabbed a rifle muzzle into his ribs . . . hard.

'Ground the long gun, private,' the sergeant brusquely ordered.

Pootes, very conscious that there were likely to be two other miscreants close by, stood in front, his Henry cocked and ready. Every sense was keenly alert, as he awaited some kind of reaction.

The prisoner, because in truth that's what he now was, stared around in pain and disbelief. He was a lean, pockmarked fellow, with lank, greasy hair and bad teeth. Far more importantly, the skin under his right eye was badly discoloured.

'Jesus, there ain't no call to go hurting me, Sarge,' he protested, still clinging to his weapon.

'Ground it!' that man barked, increasing the pressure with his rifle.

'OK, OK,' the private responded unhappily, as he swiftly placed the Springfield's butt into the mud. 'Jeez, what's all this about?' Then he saw the gun-toting civilian, and his eyes widened in surprise.

'Where are your friends?' Pootes demanded.

That was received with incredulity. 'Friends! What friends?' came the unhelpful response. 'I ain't got none, on account of most folks take agin me as soon as they get downwind.' As he spoke, his blackened teeth became ever more obvious, and as Rhodes closed in he got a whiff of deeply rancid breath.

'The two men that helped you rape my niece, up in Kentucky,' Pootes snarled. 'Where are they?'

'Whaat?' the soldier exclaimed, his eyes now like saucers.

Rhodes grabbed the suspect's rifle and sniffed the muzzle. 'This gun's been fired recently,' he accused.

The horrified private was clearly struggling to cope with such outlandish accusations. 'I fired it at the rebel fort, for Christ sake,' he protested. 'That's what we're supposed to do, ain't it? An' I ain't raped anyone, ever!' As his two captors exchanged sceptical glances, he added, 'Why pick on me, anyhu?'

'Because Martha's killer had a powder burn under his right eye, just like you,' the marshal replied. 'And someone just tried to kill me.' The incongruity of saying such a thing on a field of battle completely escaped him as he turned to the curious onlookers. 'Any of you know this man?' he demanded.

Every one of them answered with either a curt shake of the head or a blank stare. Not that that really meant anything.

'Lots of fellas got powder burns,' the thoroughly frightened private shouted, backing away from Rhodes's rifle muzzle. 'Me having one don't mean nothing.'

'We need to get him to the rear,' Pootes opined, and received a nod of agreement from the sergeant. Aiming his Henry directly at his prisoner's head, he continued, 'You try to run from me, an' I'll shoot you dead. Savvy?'

The soldier swallowed hard and nodded frantically. As he was led away, he desperately tried to think of anything that might improve his situation. Only one thing occurred to him. 'I ain't never been to Kentucky. Any part of it. Leastways not that I know of!'

'Come on Jase. You're supposed to be the brains of this outfit. Why they taking that poor sap away?'

'How the hell should I know? But I sure aim to find out. An' keep your poxy voice down!'

General Grant gratefully stepped on to the relatively substantial deck of the USS *Cincinnati*. The sweating sailors in the boat below had had a tough time of it, rowing him out to the flagship against the current, and were doubtless as glad to be rid of him as he was to vacate the little craft. As he peered around at the unfamiliar surroundings, what he now saw for the first time definitely gave him pause. It wasn't just the army that had taken losses. Two heavy guns had been upended, damaging the surrounding planking. Despite the protective iron plating, sections of timber bulwarking had been badly knocked about, and a number of bloodstains still visible on the decking confirmed the human cost of taking Fort Henry. The general possessed imagination enough to visualize the horrific injuries that could be inflicted by jagged splinters. He could only assume that the other vessels moored nearby had been similarly ill-treated.

His grim contemplation was abruptly cut short by the uncharacteristically tardy emergence of Flag Officer Andrew Hull Foote, commander of the Western Gunboat Flotilla. A grey-bearded, harassed-looking individual, he hastened over to salute his distinguished visitor. There was a deep sadness to his eyes that hinted at the reason for his enforced absence.

'My apologies for not being on deck when you arrived, General. I was checking on our casualties below. We incurred quite a butcher's bill.'

Grant, always unconcerned with formality, waved away the other man's concerns at the lack of ceremony. He also didn't want to dwell on the human cost of their triumph, because he wasn't merely there to inspect the flotilla. He had fresh orders to impart. 'My compliments on your victory, Foote. You have more than justified my confidence in you. Seeing what you have endured though, it pains me to have to tell you that I have more work for you.'

The naval officer shrugged. 'That's what we are out here for. To finish this ghastly business as soon as possible. Pray tell me what it is that you need.'

Grant smiled his appreciation. 'It is my intention to immediately turn my army to the east and attack Fort Donelson on the Cumberland River. As the crow flies, it is only some twelve miles distant, and is the last Confederate stronghold in this vicinity. I need

you to return to Cairo, collect whatever reinforcements you find there, and then steam up the
Cumberland to support my assault. If your gunboats
perform anything like as well as they have here, we
should make short work of the rebel garrison.' He
paused to chuckle at some recollection or other
before adding, 'It has to be said that General Smith
was most put out at your rapid success.'

Foote's tired features lit up with pleasure at such
fulsome praise. Unlike some of his fellow officers, he
had no concerns about cooperating fully with the
army. His genuine liking for the commanding
general only served to reinforce this attitude.
'Getting in close served us well on this occasion. If we
can do the same on the Cumberland, we might well
be able to embarrass the general again.' The
prospect of such brought a broad smile to his face.
Had he known more of what awaited him on the
other watercourse, his reaction might have been
rather more muted. . . .

'Visited with a fella who said that the law dog took his
prisoner 'cause he had a powder burn under his
right eye. Kind of makes you think, don't it?'

The three men were hunkered down within spit-
ting distance of the vanquished fort. They would
dearly have loved some hot coffee, but their chances
of getting a fire together were exceedingly slim and,
as the joke went, Slim had just left town!

With their boots permanently sodden, all they
could hope for was an order to move to higher

ground. Part of Smith's brigade had ventured into Fort Henry, but in such conditions even he could see that it made sense to leave possession of it to the navy. Why anybody had even thought of constructing such a low-lying strongpoint was beyond comprehension.

'Jesus, Jase!' Forrest blurted out. 'That means the little bitch talked, an' they know who we are.'

'That's doodly squat, Rab. If'en they did know what we all looked like they wouldn't have taken him.'

'Maybe so, or maybe that damned marshal's a right tricky cuss, an' he's trying to flush all three of us out.'

This exchange hadn't gone down well with Brin Taylor. His first real taste of action had shaken him up more than he cared to admit, and as if that wasn't enough, he now faced the prospect of being hung for something he hadn't done. It was all just too much. 'Well, I don't care two shits about any maybes,' he loudly exclaimed. 'Come nightfall I'm getting out of this army for good!'

'Nobody's going nowhere, Brin,' Metford snarled, his voice loaded with menace. 'Least of all you. We stay together and just keep our heads down. An' keep your tarnal voice low!'

Taylor shook his head adamantly. 'That don't answer any more, Jase. I didn't rape that poor girl, an' I ain't gonna swing for it. I want out of here, an' nobody's gonna stop me!'

CHAPTER FIVE

The sudden outbreak of gunfire dragged Pootes out of a light and unsettled slumber. As his eyes flitted around the tent's darkened interior, his breathing was shallow and rapid. Had the God-damned pickets truly gone mad, or what? Then, interspersed with the shooting, there came a demonic howling and a hole was torn through the canvas just above his head. It seemed that yet again someone was trying to kill him, although on this occasion it might just be the enemy alone.

Grabbing his Henry, Pootes rolled out of his bedroll on to all fours and scurried towards the tent flap. Outside, all was pandemonium. Following Fort Henry's capture, the army had gratefully moved to higher ground, but it now appeared that not all the local Confederates had surrendered. As shrieking riders galloped through the massive encampment, disconcerted bluecoats ineffectually fired their single-shot Springfields. The raiders were using pitch-coated torches to fire tents, wagons and anything else that would burn. Dazzling muzzle flashes and pockets of powder smoke only added to the inevitable confusion.

And then abruptly, the danger became very personal, and a shock of real fear beset Pootes as he spotted a sabre-wielding horseman pounding directly towards his position. Standing next to the startled marshal, a Union private instinctively levelled his long rifle and fired. Yet rather than a satisfying crash, there was merely a muted pop as the hammer struck a copper percussion cap. Either a misfire or carelessness in loading had rendered him defenceless. But not so the lawman!

Levering in a metallic cartridge from the cylindrical magazine, Pootes took rapid aim and squeezed off a shot. The bullet struck the horse in its chest, but such was its momentum that it just kept on coming, and now it was only a few yards away. Yet unlike his horrified companion, the lone civilian didn't have to frantically fiddle about with loose powder and ball: he simply worked the under lever and fired again. The doomed animal was struck once more, and this time its front legs buckled, bringing it crashing down on to a tent. Its rider also fell heavily into more canvas, but still managed to make a grab for his holstered revolver.

The befuddled infantryman was still ramming a fresh charge home, but it mattered not. With consummate ease, Pootes levered in yet another cartridge and shot their determined attacker between the eyes. His shattered skull momentarily jerked back, before the entire twitching corpse tumbled forwards, dripping blood and brain matter.

And then, as quickly as it had begun, the attack was over. Leaving burning wagons and not a few victims, the mostly triumphant Confederate cavalry raced off out of range and into the night. Yelling jubilantly, they herded a number of captured horses before them.

'Wow wee, that's one hell of a gun, mister!' exclaimed the mightily relieved private. 'You want to sell it? I'd give you my sister for it . . . if I had one!'

A quick glance at the soldier convinced Pootes that he'd probably got off lucky. 'You sound like a man mighty keen to get his hands on a repeater.'

'Why the hell not?' His new acquaintance hefted his Springfield. 'You would too, if your life depended on shit like this.'

Despite the circumstances, the lawman laughed out loud. 'Well, in that case it pains me to tell you that this here Henry just ain't for sale . . . not for anyone's sister. But mayhap there is something I can do for you.' So saying, he ambled over to his shattered victim. Grimacing with distaste, he grabbed hold of the butternut grey tunic and heaved the cadaver on to its back. Conveniently, the marshal had killed an ornately garbed officer, and there in the holster sat his prize. Nodding with satisfaction, he extracted the distinctive LeMat 'grape-shot revolver', favoured by many Southern officers, and returned to the bemused soldier.

'Here,' he said handing it over. 'You've got yourself a repeater, although I'll allow that the barrel's not as long as mine. If you're lucky you might find spare cap 'n ball in his pockets. Just don't let any of your officers see it, or they'll probably take it off you.'

The enlisted man's eyes widened expressively. 'Gee thanks, mister. For a lawman, you ain't half bad.'

'You know what I am, huh?'

'Shucks, everybody does. The news that you're hunting someone went round the camp like wild-fire.'

Pootes grunted, before answering somewhat cryptically. 'That knowledge ain't exactly produced any fruit yet, but I guess there's time.'

A non-com bellowed for the private's attention, who concealed his new acquisition before hastening to comply. Not having understood the remark, he wouldn't have known how to respond anyway.

It was shortly after first light when Sergeant Rhodes led Captain Bragg over to the marshal's tent. That individual had been unable to grab any shuteye after the attack, and so wasn't particularly feeling his best. He had never gained any pleasure from killing folks, even when they deserved it, and this particular event had preyed on his mind.

'What the hell was all that about last night?' he irritably demanded of the staff officer.

The captain glanced around and then shrugged. Smoke from some of the smouldering wagons still drifted up into the chill sky. 'Hit and run raid,' he replied. 'The Rebs are mighty good at that sort of thing. Guess they must have been pissed off at losing Fort Henry, and thought to give us some grief. They're certainly richer in horseflesh now, an' that's for sure.' His eyes abruptly settled on Pootes. 'Anyhu, that's by the by. Something else took place last night that don't sit right and I need your help.'

Despite his ill humour, the lawman felt a stir of interest. Since joining the Army of the Tennessee he had mostly, and understandably, been made to feel like an encumbrance. That seemed to be changing.

'It's been reported that a private in the 18th Illinois has been found dead,' Bragg continued. 'A couple of other men lost their lives in the raid and more than a few were wounded, but this is something different. Apparently his throat has been cut from ear to ear, very much as though he's been murdered by one of our own.'

Now that did seize the lawman's attention. He thought for a moment before posing a rather strange question. 'Was he wearing a forage cap?'

'What's that got to do with anything?'

From the saddlebags that he had retrieved from his dead horse, Pootes produced the cap found at the farm. 'This belonged to one of the rapists.'

Bragg nodded his understanding, but that was all he could supply. 'As to that, you'll need to look for yourself. I haven't seen the body, and to be honest with you, marshal, I ain't got time for any of this. The country is at war with itself, as General Smith is fond of reminding us, and this army is on the move again.'

Pootes smiled sadly. 'So you've got a murdered

soldier you don't know what to do with, and all of a sudden I might just be useful.'

The captain matched his smile. 'That's about the size of it, yeah.'

The lawman glanced briefly at Rhodes and then back to the officer. 'In that case I want something from you. I need you to assign the sergeant to me until I say otherwise.'

'Why?'

Pootes shrugged. 'He seems like a good man, and his uniform makes my job a whole lot easier.'

Bragg gazed speculatively at the startled non-com, deliberated for a moment, and then nodded again. 'Fair enough. Consider it done. Anything else before I go . . . because it appears there usually is with you?'

'The dead man. Can you hold his company back until I question them? If he was one of those I'm hunting, then the other two are probably in the same unit.'

Genuine regret appeared on the captain's bluff features. 'I can see why it would help, but I'm afraid it's too late for that. The 18th Illinois are already on the march east. Grant is a real push-hard when he's got the bit between his teeth, and he's got his sights set on another fort.'

'God damn it!' Pootes exclaimed, abruptly galvanized into action. 'Sergeant, you and me had better go inspect the body before that marches off as well!'

Bragg had a sudden thought. 'What about the private you arrested yesterday? By all accounts you put quite a scare into him.'

'Release him.'

'So soon?'

The marshal nodded. 'Call it a hunch, but I don't believe he raped anyone in Kentucky. And if he was in irons last night he certainly won't have slit anyone's throat!'

The blood-soaked body proved to be a lonely and pitiful sight. Unlike other casualties of the night attack, it had been left in plain sight, and abandoned by the rest of the regiment. Grimacing with distaste, Pootes knelt down on the grass next to it to inspect the single, gaping cut. His experienced eye told him that the killer had struck from behind and was undoubtedly right-handed, because the throat had been deeply slit from left to right. The Union blue jacket was still sodden with blood that had not yet had the chance to dry in the chill air.

'Some kind of very sharp cutting tool. Maybe a razor,' he muttered, thinking aloud. Grunting, he glanced down the length of the scrawny body, before placing his forage cap on to the corpse's head. 'Perfect fit, but it don't really mean a whole lot in the scheme of things.'

Sam Rhodes was baffled. 'Why not?'

'Because someone's already taken his rifle and his boots. Whose to say they wouldn't have taken his cap as well?' Pootes gazed bleakly around the now empty encampment. There were plenty of soldiers in the distance, but that was little consolation. 'Sweet Jesus! If we could just have got here before they left.'

'So what do we do now ... boss?' the sergeant queried with a wry smile.

Pootes's eyebrows raised in surprise. 'This could just have been a settling of scores, but my gut tells me he's one of the three cockchafers I'm after. So we follow on, of course. Oh, and since we're working together, call me either "Marshal" or "Frank". Being as that's my given name.'

'You right sure you want to do that, *Marshal?* Seems like a pretty good way to get yourself kilt, is all.'

It was the lawman's turn to smile. 'It's what we do, isn't it? You're paid to fight the Confederacy, and I'm paid to catch felons. And for me, on this occasion, it's real personal.'

Rhodes shrugged. 'Fair enough. Guess I just wanted to make sure, is all.' He paused to glance around. 'You figuring on walking like the rest of us common solders from now on?'

It was the marshal's turn to shrug. 'I don't happen to possess a spare horse. And besides, mounted I stand out a mite too much.'

Glancing off to the great body of moving infantry in the east, the sergeant squinted against the low winter sun. 'Well, in that case we'd better get moving, hadn't we?'

And so they did.

'You reckon that's him?'
  'I reckon.'
  'On foot now, huh?'

63

'That's a mighty good description of a man without a horse, Rab.'

'Shucks, Jase, you got no call to get like that. I ain't Brin, you know.'

'An' that's lucky for you, ain't it? Huh? Huh?'

'Jeez . . . ! So what do we do? About the law dog?'

'Way I see it, we still got the next move. So we bide our time an' wait for an edge. An' when we get it, he's a dead man, along with anyone with him!'

It had taken Charles Ferguson Smith nearly thirty-five years to get his single brigadier general's star, and he was inordinately proud of it. His peers all considered him to be the very epitome of what a general officer should look like. Tall and slim, with piercing blue eyes, he was a strict disciplinarian who still managed to be liked and respected by the common soldier. It was perhaps because they sensed that he knew his business, and so was less likely to be careless with their lives. Surprisingly, even though it had taken Smith such a long time to attain his rank, he felt no animosity towards the much younger Ulysses Grant, who had been placed in overall command. Perhaps it was the fact that one professional recognized the same ability and commitment in another.

The responsibilities of rank happened to be weighing on him particularly heavily that morning. He was under orders not to antagonize the population of what was nominally a border state by such things as scavenging and looting. Unfortunately, an army marches if not literally, then certainly figuratively on its stomach, and the previous night's raid had left his brigade temporarily very short of wagons and supplies. All of which meant that he would now have to do what had been expressly forbidden: to loot and scavenge. Needs must, was how he rationalized it, and it was a fact that such action had been brought on by the Confederates themselves. Yet none of this made his decision any the easier.

Sighing, he reined in his horse and turned to a nearby aide. 'Major Thomas, I require you to organize and lead a sizeable foraging party.' As that man's eyebrows rose in surprise, Smith added, 'Regrettable I know, but for the time being we have no choice other than to live off the land. But you are to keep force to a minimum, so choose reliable officers to assist you.' He paused before adding with great emphasis: 'The enlisted men are to be kept on a tight leash. Do you understand?'

The officer knew better than to dispute any of that. 'I do Sir,' he replied, and after saluting smartly, quickly moved off to obey.

This forward brigade of Grant's army was advancing behind a screen of cavalry through lush, open countryside. Even though it was still winter, there could be no disguising the fact that this land was ripe for the picking . . . for those so inclined. On either flank of the line of march, timber farmhouses standing alongside sturdy barns were visible. There was definitely a case to be made that the populace had more than it needed, whilst the Union Army had less than it wanted!

Yet General Smith watched with mixed feelings as companies of men with fixed bayonets fanned out to the south. The rebels had undoubtedly brought this on themselves by attempting to secede from the United States, but he had little stomach for making war on women and children. The direction taken by the foragers was a deliberate precaution to avoid any of his men inadvertently straying north of the border into Kentucky.

'I want no unnecessary bloodshed!' he bellowed out to the departing major, who acknowledged the command with a wave. From then on, whatever took place was effectively out of the general's control . . . and he had seen enough of warfare to know that!

Ezra Martin viewed the distant figures with justifiable alarm. Although not a slaveholder, he was a prosperous second-generation farmer with a great deal to lose. His substantial two-storey house was enviably well furnished. Although nothing like as grand as the great plantation mansions in states such as Virginia or the Carolinas, it was still a very impressive property. But it wasn't inanimate possessions that concerned him the most. He owned a great many cattle, which were bound to be of interest to the northern invaders. Even more important were the two daughters anxiously watching beside him.

'What are you going to do, Pa?' Jessie queried anxiously. She was eighteen, blonde, blue-eyed, and even though he said it himself, gorgeous.

'To them, nothing,' he bleakly responded. 'There's a whole army out there, an' I ain't doing anything that'll provoke them. What you and your sister will do is go down to the cellar and hide behind the barrels. Pull some old rags over you and keep silent . . . whatever happens. An' if your mother was still alive, God bless her, she'd be going with you, because I know what soldiers are capable of.'

Jessie and her equally attractive sibling, Sarah, stared at him wide-eyed for a moment before hurrying off to comply. 'Remember,' he barked after them, more harshly than he had intended. 'Don't come out until I say!'

Faced with great alluring swathes of countryside, Major Thomas's foragers had split up into units of roughly ten men commanded by a non-com or junior officer. Considering his superior's strict orders, it wasn't an ideal situation, but there were many hungry soldiers to be fed and he had no intention of disappointing them.

It was one of these groups that now approached the Martin farm. Mindful of the previous night's attack, they had their rifles ready, although no one really expected trouble. After all, it was daylight, the army was on the move, and their own cavalry was out in force.

'Will you just look at this place,' one of the privates exclaimed. He hailed from a northern industrial city, full of squalor and filth. 'There must be an awful lot of something in a palace like that.'

'We're here for food, not loot,' his sergeant retorted.

'They're rebs, ain't they?' snarled Jason Metford. 'It was rebs kilt a buddy of ours in that raid last night. Bastards cut him another mouth. A better man you couldn't have hoped to come across.'

'That's damn right!' Rab Forrest affirmed. 'He was like a brother to us, and I say we make this southern trash pay. A spread like this must have way more than just cattle.'

Uncertainty began to register on the young sergeant's features. Promoted beyond his abilities in a constantly expanding army, he hadn't yet learned that it was a mistake to curry favour with his subordinates. Such behaviour merely indicated weakness. But it was also true that he had little sympathy for secessionists. Yeah, he'd heard the major's orders, but where was Thomas now? 'I suppose it wouldn't hurt to take a look inside,' he reluctantly opined.

'Now that's more like it,' one of the other privates gleefully remarked.

At that moment, the door to the farmhouse opened and Ezra Martin appeared, his hands empty and held away from his body. Walking out on to the front porch, he calmly surveyed the trespassers. 'Behind this house you will find a herd of dairy cattle. Take as many as you need. No one will hinder you. We don't want any trouble.'

Metford didn't even bother glancing at the sergeant before he stepped forward, his fixed bayonet glinting dangerously in the sunlight. He had instinctively taken charge, and the others recognized the fact. 'Well, trouble has come to you, mister, whether you like it or not. So step aside, before this toad stabber separates your ribs!'

Martin, a broad-shouldered individual in his early forties, stared at the threatening point for a long moment. His strong jaw worked slowly, as though chewing tobacco. Part of him desperately wanted to resist, but then common sense took hold. He had instructed all his employees to scatter, and so was the only man left. Getting himself killed and leaving his daughters without a parent would achieve nothing. Slowly and very reluctantly, he did as instructed.

'Now that wasn't so hard, was it?' Metford crowed triumphantly. Suddenly charged with anticipation, he surged across the threshold, before abruptly stopping to glance back at Forrest. Winking broadly, he remarked, 'Who knows? We might just get lucky!'

CHAPTER SIX

As Jessie and Sarah heard the multitude of heavy boots on the floorboards above, their blood ran cold, because they immediately realized that the footwear didn't belong to either their father or any of the field hands. With the light too poor for either to make out the other's expression, their searching fingers reached out for the solace of human contact.

'I'm scared,' Jessie whispered timidly from under the sacking. 'What should we do?'

Sarah didn't even have to think about that. 'You heard what Pa said,' she hissed, squeezing her sister's hand reassuringly. 'We stay hidden until he tells us different.'

When it came to doing wrong, Metford was as sharp as the razor he had killed Brin Taylor with. He knew immediately that something wasn't right underfoot. Sections of the boarding sounded far too hollow.

'What's 'neath this floor?' he demanded, as other soldiers noisily crowded into the house behind him.

Ezra Martin's features remained deadpan only with great difficulty. 'Nothing,' he affirmed. 'The land hereabouts gets too boggy for cellars and the like.'

'Is that a fact?' Metford sneered. 'Well, we've just come from taking your Fort Henry, where our boots never dried out. Now *that* was boggy!' Glancing at the thick rug before him he added, 'Rab, how's about shifting that for me?'

Immediately recognizing the possibilities, Forrest seized the covering and pulled it to one side. There, for all to see, was a hinged trapdoor that drew knowing smiles from the Union men.

'No cellars, huh?' Metford crowed as he cocked his rifle. Mindful of hidden dangers, the others did the same. As Forrest cautiously lifted the door by its recessed latch, all of them kept their distance from the gaping void.

'Who all's down there?' Metford demanded. 'Show yourself, or we'll turn your night into day.'

'Night into day,' repeated one of the dimmer soldiery. 'What the hell's he mean by that?'

'There's no one down there,' Ezra Martin protested. 'We just use it as a grain store, is all.'

'*We*,' Metford barked. 'Whose *we*? Spread like this must support a lot of folks, yet so far all we've seen is you.'

Despite his concerns, Martin's self-control was beginning to slip. What right did this trash have to make demands when they were on *his* property? 'I sent them all running to avoid you lawless scav-

71

engers,' he stridently replied, all the while wishing that he had let his girls take their chances in the fields as well.

'Scavengers, huh?' sneered Metford, swinging his bayonet over to cover the irate farmer. 'Rab, get one of those lamps lit, pronto.'

'Let's just forget all this an' take the cattle,' the sergeant optimistically ordered, but no one was listening.

It was the lighting of one of his own kerosene lamps by Rab Forrest that effectively pushed the farmer over the brink, because he knew that it might not be intended solely for illumination. As the flickering lamp was carried perilously close to the cellar hatch, something snapped within him. With a great roar of anger, Martin violently shoved Metford's Springfield to one side with his left hand, whilst at the same time drawing a single-shot Derringer from behind his back.

An entirely welcome, but unintended consequence of the former action was that the bayonet tip sliced deeply through the ineffectual sergeant's right cheek. As blood flowed from the nasty wound, that man howled with agony and staggered back towards the threshold. Any control that he might have exerted over his men was inextricably lost.

Martin cocked the diminutive pistol and took rapid aim at Forrest. Yet just as he squeezed the trigger, another luckless private stumbled in front of the muzzle. The 'stocking pistol' as it was sometimes known, crashed out in the enclosed space, sending its .41 calibre ball into that man's chest. More screams and a cloud of powder smoke all added to the abrupt chaos in the crowded room.

Cursing his bad luck, Martin drew the Derringer's companion piece with his left hand and tried again. All he could think of was preventing the lamp from being dropped into the cellar, and with his mortally wounded victim now on the floor out of the way he would get another chance.

Forrest, strangely unaware that he was the sole focus of a desperate parent's rage, was gripped by indecision. Still clutching the kerosene lamp, he didn't know whether to heave it through the hatch or stand off. Only dimly did he then perceive the second Derringer lining up on him, and that belated recognition wouldn't be enough to save him.

Metford's natural aggression meant that he ignored the wounded non-com and swung his rifle back towards his assailant. Its long barrel whacked into Martin's shoulder just as he squeezed the trigger. The lead ball still struck its intended target, but only to wound rather than kill.

As dreadful pain engulfed his left arm, Forrest swung round and momentarily lost his balance. In a desperate bid to avoid tumbling into the cellar, he let go of the heavy lamp and managed to stagger clear. The incendiary device plummeted to the solid floor below and immediately burst into flames. Fuelled by the highly flammable liquid, they rapidly spread.

The resulting screams from the cellar only served to galvanize Martin to greater frenzy. Dropping his empty firearms, he seized hold of Metford's rifle and wrestled him backwards. It would likely have gone badly for the soldier, except that the foragers' superior numbers finally began to make a difference. One of them plunged his spike bayonet into the farmer's unprotected belly, and viciously twisted it for good measure. Even as the southerner roared with agony, another length of iron penetrated his chest, effectively ending any resistance.

With blood frothing from his lips, Ezra Martin sank to his knees. As he did so, his pain-filled eyes settled on the flames emanating from the cellar. The wailing from his beloved daughters only added to his dreadful suffering, but that was to be short-lived. His torso drenched in blood, the farmer collapsed sideways and choked on his last breath.

'Who told you to throw that lamp?' Metford hollered at his wounded crony accusingly. 'Them gals is no use to us burnt to a crisp! This son of a bitch wouldn't have hidden them if they weren't mighty purdy.'

Forrest was hurting too bad to respond to that, but one of the others discarded his rifle and made for the cellar stairs. But he got no further than the top of them, because the kerosene-assisted fire was spreading rapidly.

'For God's sake help us!' shrieked a female voice.

With the timber building most certainly doomed, Metford was losing interest in the whole business. 'He's the only one likely to,' he yelled back. 'Because we sure as hell can't.' Without any apparent remorse he turned to leave. Only the process of looting Martin's pockets of a surprisingly agreeable number of Yankee dollars delayed his departure.

Once outside, he found the ineffectual sergeant on the ground, moaning and holding his badly gashed cheek. If he was to stand any chance of regaining his looks, a flap of sliced skin urgently required stitching. Nearby was a sturdy farm wagon that would have been useful for carrying off any spoils. As it was, Metford's quick wits swiftly saw another use for it. A way perhaps of finally shaking off the lawman that had been dogging their footsteps for more than long enough without actually having to kill him. For his plan to work though, would require him to begin demonstrating some unaccustomed concern for his fellow man.

'Forget the house!' he bellowed at his companions. 'There's nothing we can do for it . . . even if we wanted.'

As the Union squad straggled back outside, with two of their number assisting Forrest, it was evident that some of them were very discontented with the bloody turn of events. 'It ain't right what's happening to them females,' one of them protested. 'It ain't right at all. I mean, Christ, they're gonna burn to death!'

'What ain't right is the waste of some prime ass, but if you're so all fired unhappy go back in there and get them,' Metford retorted harshly. 'But think on this. They're the enemy. Them an' their pa. An' 'cause of him, we got one man dead an' two injured.

It's these fellas we should be thinking on.'

'If I don't get some doctoring I'll likely bleed to death,' mumbled the sergeant pitifully, thereby playing into Metford's hands.

'Hitch a team to the wagon,' that man ordered, before hastening over to his wounded 'friend'. 'Come on pard. I'm gonna get you an' the sergeant to a sawbones. It's the least I can do.'

There followed a period of manic activity, as some of the men located a couple of mules, and only with great difficulty managed to harness them to the wagon. And all the while, the fire spread into the main building, sending up great clouds of smoke that would be visible for miles around. Screams, first of terror and then of agony, came from the cellar, until after a time there was silence save for the crackling of burning timbers. With it came a faint sickly smell of burning flesh, drifting over on the light wind.

As the fire engulfed the entire structure, the heat became unbearable. It was definitely time to go. The two wounded men were assisted on to the wagon, under the reproachful stares of Martin's farmhands who had gathered some distance away. Under closer examination, Forrest only had a flesh wound in the meaty part of his left arm. Yet the amount of blood spilt was quite impressive and would likely fool anyone outside the medical profession. The sergeant, who now held a grubby kerchief against his very painful facial injury, began to rock to and fro on the wagon bed, muttering unintelligibly.

It was inevitable that the inferno would attract unwelcome attention, and it duly arrived in the form of Major Thomas and a small detachment of cavalry. Almost apoplectic with rage, that officer sharply reined in his mount and gazed around at the scattered remnants of the foraging party.

'What the devil have you God-damn blockheads done?' he demanded shrilly. 'I'll have you all bucked and gagged for this. Why is this house afire? I ordered no violence against civilians.' It all came out so fast as to be almost incoherent.

Since any response from the badly hurting sergeant would have been equally garbled, it was left to Metford to respond. 'The farmer pulled a couple of purse cannons from his britches and went plumb loco. Kilt one man and badly wounded these two others . . . sir.'

The major stared at him incredulously. 'One man attacked all of you. Now why would he do a fool thing like that?'

Whilst the others appeared uncomfortable, Metford just shrugged. 'Guess he just didn't take to Union men driving off his cattle, Major. That's what we were fixing to do . . . as ordered.' He deliberately let those two words hang in the air.

Thomas viewed the lean, powder-marked private with vague distaste. There was something about the man that set him on edge. And yet there was obviously some substance to his words, because two men *were* injured for all to see. The major's nose abruptly twitched. 'What's that strange stink?' he demanded.

'Not every soul made it out of the house, sir,' Metford matter-of-factly replied.

Thomas's eyes became like saucers, and abruptly he wanted to be away from this charnel house. Turning to the cavalry, he barked, 'You men, drive those cattle back to the main column. You foragers, make your way back there at best speed. You've done more than enough for one day.' That last remark was liberally laced with sarcasm that was likely wasted on most of them.

Metford seized his chance. 'The sergeant's hurt real bad, sir. Figured I'd use this wagon to take both wounded over to the surgeon. With your permission, sir.' The scheming private had carefully avoided stating *which* surgeon.

Thomas was already urging his horse away. 'Yes, yes. Do whatever you need to.' And with that he was off, hurriedly escaping a particularly unpleasant face of war. It had already occurred to him that he wouldn't have been the only officer to spot the smoke, and that he might well have to endure some awkward questions from General Smith.

'I'll be right honest with you, Sergeant, I ain't used to this walking shit.'

Rhodes chuckled. With the unfamiliar burden of rifle, bedroll and saddlebags, the marshal was quite obviously making heavy weather of it. So what they saw next immediately made Pootes envious. Some distance ahead, on their right flank, they spotted a wagon approaching pulled by two mules. As it rattled nearer, it became apparent that its three occupants all wore Union blue. One sat on the bench seat, controlling the team, whilst the others were in the back.

'They've got the right idea. They're just going the wrong way, is all,' Pootes muttered sourly. Both men continued to watch the conveyance as it drew parallel some one hundred yards distant.

'Now why would they be heading back to the river?' the sergeant pondered. Cupping his hands, he bellowed out, 'You there. What's your business?'

Strangely, the teamster didn't even turn to look at them. Instead he pulled the peak of his forage cap down lower and stared fixedly ahead. Then he merely proffered a casual wave before urging the mules to greater speed.

'Bastards!' Rhodes exclaimed. 'They're up to something an' no mistake, but short of popping a cap on them there ain't a whole lot I can do.'

Temporarily losing interest in the wagon, Pootes scrutinized the horizon ahead. Despite his being footsore and markedly slower than his companion, the two of them still appeared to be closing on the main force, and the reason for that soon became obvious. Considering the season, the landscape was still amazingly lush. Tennessee was obviously a bountiful state, and from the number of foragers on the move it seemed that General Smith was taking advantage of the fact.

It was then that the teamster's unnaturally rigid demeanour returned to trouble the lawman, because suspicion of everyone and everything was the nature of his job. He took another look at the retreating wagon. Why would the soldier studiously avoid looking at them, and yet still acknowledge their presence? It didn't make sense . . . unless he didn't want his face to be seen!

The temporary teamster heaved a great sigh of relief as he finally reined in the mule team outside the surgeon's tent. Locating the field hospital had been easy, because not even a blind man on a galloping horse could miss the large bucket of bloody severed limbs awaiting disposal. There were two large tents, presumably for the convalescing wounded, and a smaller one where the sawing and stitching undoubtedly took place.

Metford's release of tension was due to his belief that he had shaken off the 'law dog' once and for all. He had been severely tempted to take a pot shot at him from the wagon as they almost crossed paths, but the marshal was no longer alone, and the mule team would have made an easy target. And besides, they were going in opposite directions, so it really didn't matter any more. All he had to do now was divest himself of the wounded and disappear. He had had a bellyful of Grant's army, and because he was fighting for personal gain rather than to end the evil of slavery, he would simply do the same as a great many others: desert, and then sign up for another cash bounty with a different regiment. Until then, the money that he had taken from the rebel farmer would easily see him through.

For a long moment he scrutinized his surroundings. With Smith's men on their way to the Cumberland River, the vast encampment was considerably reduced but still sizeable. Although the private couldn't know it, General Grant was in no all-fired hurry to move, because there would be no assault on Fort Donelson without the navy's heavy guns. And since the gunboats had to carry out repairs and then steam some considerable distance north on the Tennessee before then returning southeast on the Cumberland, the rest of the army could take its sweet time.

'If you don't get me to the sawbones, I'm gonna bleed to death sure as shooting,' Forrest bleated from the rear of the wagon.

Metford sighed again, only this time with impatience. He surely wasn't cut out for this nurse-maiding shit! 'Just hush your mouth, Rab, while I take a looksee,' he snapped.

Inside his operating tent, an extremely weary surgeon captain regarded the new arrival with undisguised dismay . . . until he realized that the soldier wasn't wounded. 'Only the dead and dying are welcome in here, Private,' he caustically remarked. 'You look too damned healthy to me.'

Metford executed a sketchy salute before gesturing outside. 'Got a couple of wounded men in the back of the wagon, sir. Be obliged if you'd look to them.'

The bearded, bloodstained surgeon gazed at him curiously. 'My last casualties came from that little fracas in the night. To my knowledge there ain't been any fighting around here since then.'

The enlisted man felt a tightening in his stomach as it abruptly occurred to him that he might well need to be careful with this poxy officer. 'We were with a foraging party off to the east, when some God-damned farmer tried to parole us all to Jesus.'

Surgeon Captain Tobias Reynold's eyes narrowed. 'With Smith's men? So why not take them to one of *his* field surgeons?'

'Tried that, sir. But I couldn't find any.'

The other man regarded him with obvious suspicion, but then a plaintive cry from the wagon cut short any more discourse. 'So get them in here!' he snapped, before calling to one of his assistants. 'We've got some more customers, Taylor. Rouse yourself.'

Metford helped the sergeant in first. He was faint with blood loss and shock, and did actually seem to be in a bad way. It was only after the increasingly edgy private had got Forrest into the tent and was then beginning to sidle back towards the open flap that he realized he had a real problem.

'You stay right where you are, soldier,' Reynolds barked at the clearly restless man, before turning his attention to his patients.

It was some time before the 'sawbones' paid any more attention to Jason Metford, and when he did the dialogue began fairly innocuously. 'The sergeant is badly injured. He'll be staying in my care for some time. . . unless infection sets in,' he added ominously. 'This other fellow has only a minor flesh wound. Light duties for a few days should see him right.'

Metford patted Forrest companionably on his *right* shoulder. 'Well then, Rab, looks like we can be on our way.'

'To where?' the officer queried in apparent innocence.

'Wherever the 18th Illinois ends up, I guess,' the other responded lightly.

The surgeon captain was primarily a medical man, but he was also a soldier. And that latter part of him insisted that this particular private was undoubtedly a dodgy character who had little intention of returning to his unit. An idea abruptly came to him that made him chuckle for the first time in many a day. 'Come with me!' he peremptorily commanded.

With Forrest following on in an uncomprehending daze, and his 'friend' carrying both their Springfields, the officer led the two enlisted men outside and on across the trampled grass towards the river. As Metford took in the squat, potent-looking ironclad moored in the centre of the watercourse, his heart sank. This was indeed an ominous turn of events.

Without any hesitation, Reynolds hollered over to the gunboat in surprisingly flowery language, as though he was taking great pleasure in the situation. 'My compliments to the officer of the watch. If you would oblige me, I have here two eager and intrepid voyagers seeking passage to Fort Donelson.'

Someone in officer's uniform answered that with a friendly wave, and a short while later a rowing boat headed over to the riverbank. Whilst this was happening, the surgeon turned to consider the two privates. His patient, weary from blood loss, appeared unconcerned at the prospect of a boat ride – but not so the other. His expression displayed barely concealed rage.

'Don't fret, soldier,' the officer blandly remarked. 'In a way I'm doing you a favour. Think of all the walking and possible blisters I've saved you. Your destination lies on the Cumberland River, and that is where this boat is bound. I treated a number of their sailors after the attack on Fort Henry, so I'm sure they'll be happy to do me a favour and accommodate you both.'

And so it transpired. As Surgeon Reynolds walked slowly back to his field hospital, having observed the two infantrymen being rowed away like 'pressed men' of old, he laughed long and heartily. Modern bloody warfare offered little to smile about, but the sight of that potential deserter being carried off to sea, so to speak, had definitely tickled his funny bone!

Major Thomas glared at the infantry sergeant, as that man doggedly persevered with his questions. The advance force of Grant's Army of the Tennessee had made camp for the night. It had been a long day, but at least the following one would likely see them reaching their next destination. Greatly strengthened pickets had been established to deter another night attack, and the major was desperate for some shuteye. And yet here he was being pestered over the admittedly odd direction taken by a single wagon!

'Can you remember anything unusual about the men in the wagon, sir?' Rhodes persisted.

Thomas abruptly decided that enough was enough. He'd already endured a tongue lashing from old General Smith, who along with everyone else that afternoon had seen the farmhouse burning to the south. Yawning pointedly, he remarked, 'Take a hint, Sergeant, and leave me be. I ain't got either the time or the inclination for any more of your questions. Understand?'

Frank Pootes had also heard more than enough. And he for one didn't have to defer to any damned stuffed shirt. Stepping out of the shadows, he made sure that his badge of office was clearly visible in the firelight. 'I'm the United States Marshal you probably heard about. The sergeant works for me until I say otherwise. With General Grant's agreement, I'm hunting a couple of murdering rapists that are giving the Union a bad name. There *were* three of the bastards, but one of them got his throat slit last night.' His eyes like flints, Pootes let all that sink in before getting to the crux of the matter. 'Now I want an answer to the question that this man just put to you, an' you're gonna supply it. Otherwise I'll haul your ass all the way back to Grant's headquarters and tell him about your lack of cooperation. Which'll it be?'

Like most regular officers in the midst of an army, Thomas was not used to being challenged unless it was by someone of higher military rank. His eyes widened in surprise at the other's brusque tone. And yet there was something about the lawman that commanded respect. He was obviously used to confrontation, and had also employed Grant's name to great effect. Perhaps after all it might be better to humour him.

'OK, OK. I remember the man,' the major acknowledged. 'There had been an excessive amount of violence employed on a rebel farm. People had been killed, and a house burned down. This private seemed like an awkward cuss, with all the answers and trouble writ large on his face. He was supposed to take the wounded to the nearest field surgeon, not back to the Tennessee River. And one thing did stand out. He had a large powder burn under his right eye.'

'Son of a bitch!' the lawman exclaimed. 'It was him. I'd stake my saddle on it . . . wherever the hell that is now.' Glancing at the non-com he added, 'Damn shame you didn't unload that long gun on him when we had the chance.'

The bemused officer stifled another yawn with difficulty. 'So if that's all. . . .'

Pootes favoured him with the makings of a smile. 'From one federal officer to another, I thank you for that, Major. Now go get some sleep. You look plumb tuckered out.'

'Now what do we do?' Rhodes queried as they walked away.

That elicited a full-bore smile from the marshal. 'I'm gonna visit with General Smith. Reckon he'll happily hand over a couple of horses just to be rid of me.'

CHAPTER SEVEN

The new dawn found Frank Pootes and Sam Rhodes mounted and riding fast for the Tennessee River. As the marshal had surmised, General Smith had indeed considered the loss of two horses a worthwhile price to pay to be rid of an annoying civilian, who had no business to be on any battlefield.

'That pus weasel could be anywhere by now,' Rhodes opined. 'Any idea where to start looking?'

'He had wounded men in that wagon,' the marshal replied. 'So whatever answers as a sawbones in your army is where we start.'

Surgeon Reynolds viewed the two approaching riders curiously. Not having any prospective customers for the dreaded bone saw, he was sitting on an upturned bucket outside his tent, quietly enjoying a well-earned Daniel Webster cigar. What made the horsemen unusual was that one of them was a civilian. Then he spotted the federal marshal's badge, and his interest was well and truly engaged, because unlike most of the men in Grant's army he hadn't heard talk of the federal officer's mission.

'As far as I know there has been no unlawful discharge of firearms for at least twenty-four hours,' the captain drolly remarked as the two men reined in before him.

Pootes grunted. 'Very funny, I'm sure. If I had more time, I'd love to bandy words with you, but I don't. So here's the thing. We're seeking a mean-looking cuss with a powder burn under his right eye. Last we saw of him he was driving a farm wagon with two wounded men in the back.'

Inhalation of cigar smoke had nothing to do with Reynolds feeling abruptly queasy. 'What's he done amiss, Marshal?'

'I'm pretty damn sure it was him raped my niece to death in Kentucky,' Pootes grimly replied.

Although no stranger to extreme suffering and death, the surgeon's jaw noticeably tightened for a moment. 'Well then, I am mortified to inform you that I aided his swift departure, for he and his accomplice are on a gunboat speeding down the Tennessee. It seemed like a good way to keep him from deserting. He had the look of a man who might do that . . . and a great many other things besides.'

Pootes didn't even have to think about it. 'Then we, too, need to be on a gunboat. Can you assist us?'

The surgeon jumped to his feet. Here was his chance to make amends. 'You're in luck. If it can be called that. The rest of the army moves east today, and there is one gunboat left on this stretch of river.

The USS *Tyler*. I treated its captain for a splinter wound. Get your possibles and follow me.'

The last time Reynolds had arranged passage for two on a gunboat, he had walked away laughing. Now, as he watched the marshal shoulder his saddle-bags, he felt only regret. There would definitely be no levity on this occasion!

For the second time that morning, black smoke ceased to belch out of the twin stacks, and unlike the previous occasion this situation had an air of permanence about it.

'God damn it all to hell!' bellowed an individual sporting the peak cap with small gilt anchor that denoted an officer. And an angry one at that. 'Why here? Why now?' For long moments he glared helplessly at the offending yellow-banded smoke stacks, before ordering, 'Drop anchor!' Then, without waiting to see his command obeyed, he hurriedly disappeared down into the bowels of the boat. It was beyond his comprehension how *both* steam engines could cease to function at the same time!

Jason Metford raised himself up off the timber deck and cautiously glanced around. Since being brought aboard the previous afternoon, he and his listless companion had been left pretty much to their own devices. The flesh wound had left Rab Forrest strangely subdued – unaccountably so, in Metford's view, but thus far he hadn't possessed the inclination to press the matter. In an alien environment, and with nothing to occupy them, he too felt off kilter. Now and then he caught the use of strange words like 'aft' and 'stern', and briefly wondered what on earth they could mean. The quietest part of the ship, or boat, or whatever the hell it was that they were on, seemed to be at the back of it, and so that was where they had remained, mostly ignored by the surprisingly large crew.

In truth, things could have been far worse. As that poxy sawbones had promised, they no longer had to march anywhere, and the setting was undeniably tranquil. Both riverbanks were lined with oak trees, and even though the engines had unaccountably stopped again, there was enough of a current to keep the craft moving. All of which begged a question.

As a likely more approachable junior rating came close, Metford hissed out, 'Why drop anchor? Why not just go with the flow?'

The young sailor regarded the 'landlubber' with obvious pity. 'Because this boat won't manoeuvre worth a damn without the engines, that's why. Its shallow draft means it'll likely plough on into a bank. And this captain being new an' all, he can't take the chance.'

An authoritative voice yelled out, 'Move yourself, Perkins. Don't make me have to give two hollers!'

And so the fresh-faced young fellow, distinctive in his nautical leggings and blue jumper, quickly turned away from the two idlers. At that instant there came a sharp crack on the left bank, and Perkins executed an ungainly pirouette before crashing to the deck. With blood and brain matter spewing from his shattered skull, he was quite obviously beyond help.

'Sharpshooters in the trees!' shouted a petty officer, before adding somewhat superfluously, 'Take cover!'

With devilishly bad timing, that instruction came at the same time as the release of both fore and aft anchors. The USS *Pittsburgh* therefore came to a juddering halt directly opposite a veritable hornets' nest of rebels. As if to confirm this, more shots rang out in the trees. Most of the bullets ricocheted off the sloping side armour, but one struck a luckless sailor in his lower jaw, bloodily removing several teeth and pitching him backwards.

Then, with every man safely below the level of the waist-high iron bulwark, an unnatural silence fell over the boat. This was broken by the return of the now sweating and red-faced officer who appeared to Metford to be in charge. Seeing the two casualties, he reacted in a way predictable to anyone under attack: 'Run out the port side guns!'

From below, there came ominous creaking sounds as four heavy gun ports were raised. Under normal circumstances, infantry armed only with Enfield rifles would have stood little or no chance against a naval broadside. Unfortunately there was nothing normal about this situation. With the boat effectively immobile, there was very little lateral movement available to the massive smoothbore Dahlgrens. Which meant that, so long as the Confederates could move freely from behind one tree to the next, the Union gunners had no hope in hell of hitting them. But of course they were under orders to try, and

91

some of them would die in the attempt, because the best of the grey-clad marksmen had been waiting eagerly for the gunports to open.

The crash of rifles along the bank translated to screams below deck, as a number of gunners were ruthlessly picked off. Then there was a shouted order, followed by the shattering roar of four big guns discharging. Savage recoil had the boat lurching against its anchors, and the entire port side was temporarily wreathed in acrid powder smoke. The solid shot smashed into timber, bringing down branches, but entirely failing to harm any rebels, who had, of course, moved clear of the line of fire. Then, as though taunting Union impotence, their Minie bullets again tore into flesh and blood on the gun deck.

The boat's red-faced commander, going by the name of Lieutenant Leonard Paulding USN, was now only too aware of his fatal error of judgement, and angrily bellowed out, 'Lower the gun ports and secure the guns!' His order was repeated below, and soon the gun deck returned to its habitual gloom, with no artificial light permitted due to the risk of igniting the powder charges.

The knowledge that even the more sensible use of grape shot would have been unlikely to alter the result was little consolation to the officer's tortured soul. Until the equally unhappy engineer could fix the engine, Paulding's lone craft was very definitely between a rock and a hard place. Even when they were able to get up steam again, raising the anchors would involve his crew showing themselves above the level of the bulwark. And the service issue Colt Navy that he had retrieved from his cabin was unlikely to deter their assailants.

As though personally taunting him, the Confederates began hooting and hollering. It was very obvious that although the loss of Fort Henry had removed a major strongpoint, the rebels still possessed the ability to launch 'hit and run' raids and to attack isolated units.

Plagued by the indignity of being unable to stand tall on his own deck, and painfully aware that he was very likely the sole focus of those crouching on it, the young officer desperately tried to think of a way out of their awful predicament. The USS *Pittsburgh* had left Cairo with two hundred and fifty-one officers and men. That number had been reduced slightly in front of Fort Henry, but this encounter with the enemy was shaping up to be far worse. He needed no reminding that this was his first command . . . and might well be his last. The only saving grace was that Flag Officer Foote hadn't been on hand to witness the debacle!

'Excuse me, your honour.'

Paulding blinked in surprise and twisted around to peer aft. The unsolicited remark could only have come from one of the scrofulous infantry privates that he had agreed to take on board. 'I'm a naval officer, not a town mayor,' he barked. 'If you *must* talk to me, then you will address me as "sir".'

A chill cloud passed over Metford's eyes, but he

managed a passable salute before responding. 'Well hell, *sir*, I meant no offence.' Then he gestured towards the riverbank. 'Only the way I see it, you need something more than a revolver to take the starch out of their hides.' Patting his rifle, he added, 'This'll answer.'

Paulding stared at him in astonishment for a moment. Could this be the lifeline that he so urgently needed? There was only one way to find out. 'Very well, soldier,' he suddenly answered decisively. 'Show me what you can do.'

Metford smiled obliquely. He didn't do anything for nothing, but putting on a fine show for this arrogant cockchafer might well benefit him later. 'Come on, you lazy bastard,' he muttered to Forrest. 'We got work to do.'

That man showed little or no enthusiasm. 'I can't fire no long gun,' he whined. 'My arm still pains me.'

'Well, you can reload for me, can't you?' Metford snarled, grabbing both Springfields. 'Follow me!' So saying, he scrabbled over to the port-side bulwark, where he got on to his knees and peered cautiously over it into the trees.

With nothing to fire at, the Confederates had gone quiet, but they were still out there all right. And even though Metford was only a disaffected private, he possessed the tactical sense to realize that there was little point in blazing away for the sake of it. There needed to be a specific goal . . . along with a diversion. And, conveniently, the soldier didn't have long to wait.

As though by divine timing, an engine below coughed into life, and smoke again began to gush from the vertical stacks. Paulding had been impatiently waiting for his passengers to demonstrate their marksmanship, but now he suddenly understood Metford's hesitation. Glancing at the iron capstans fore and aft, the lieutenant called out, 'My men will need covering fire when they hoist the anchors.'

'They'll get it . . . sir,' the soldier retorted.

The boat's captain called out to the various ratings crouched on the deck. 'When the steam whistle sounds, take your places on the capstans and push like hell!' Then he scuttled over to the wheelhouse amidships.

Metford cocked his piece and took a deep, steadying breath, before snatching a quick look over the side. The rebels, untroubled by retaliatory gunfire, had grown overly confident. A fair few of them were in plain sight amongst the trees, and he fully intended to make them suffer for their presumption.

A shrill whistle blasted out from above the wheelhouse, and the deck was abruptly alive with sailors running for the capstans. Metford lifted the Springfield to his shoulder and drew a rapid bead on an unsuspecting enemy. At such range he had no need of the flip-up rear leaf sight. Even as he squeezed the trigger, the soldier knew that his aim was true. As his shoulder absorbed the recoil, the heavy lead ball smashed into the man's torso, knocking back him off his feet. First blood to the Yankee

. . . in this latest set-to, anyway.

With the rebels spread out along the bank and aiming at the sailors, they didn't immediately realize that they were now under accurate fire. Without even glancing back, Metford handed his empty rifle to Forrest and took aim with the other. The grey-clad enemy began firing at those unfortunates straining to lift the anchor. One on each capstan screamed out before falling away from the heavy bars. Then the Union soldier fired again. It was a peach of a shot, taking his victim between the eyes, and snuffing out his life in a spectacularly bloody fashion.

As Metford swapped long guns with his reluctant loader, the Confederate leader finally became aware that they were no longer having it all their own way. He spotted the Springfield's muzzle extending over the bulwark and bellowed out a warning to his men. Most of them stepped sharply back behind cover, but one of them wasn't quite fast enough. With a cold smile playing on his features, the marksman quite deliberately placed a heavy bullet into the man's belly. He knew full well that his anguished prey would be a long time dying, and would require the assistance of his comrades. Grimly satisfied, he ducked down behind the armoured bulwark and told Forrest to follow him along the deck. With his lethal presence now known, it made sense to move after each shot.

With most of the enemy lead now smacking into the side armour, the ratings were free to raise the anchors. As they heaved against the capstan bars, Metford again swung his rifle over the bulwark.

Although having shifted position, a blast of pressure erupted near his right ear. That had been too damn close. He fired into the trees and then again dropped out of sight.

'How's about a little help, *sir*?' he yelled over at the St Louis's captain. 'That Colt of yourn could distract them, an' give me an edge.'

Despite the fraught circumstances, Paulding twitched with distaste. He plainly wasn't used to being addressed in that fashion by one of the other ranks. Before he could reply, however, he was given something else to think on.

'The anchor's caught on something, sir,' bellowed a petty officer overseeing the rear capstan.

Ignoring the danger from the trees, Paulding leapt to his feet and ran to the stern. Even as he did so, the gunboat's bow began to shift with the current. That particular anchor was obviously clear of the riverbed. 'Put your backs into it, men!' he urged the straining men. 'One good heave and we'll be free.'

And yet it wasn't to be. Try as they might, the anchor appeared to be stuck fast. Then one of the ratings was struck in his right shoulder and fell away from his position. With fear and despondency beginning to set in, his comrades abruptly flagged in their efforts.

Metford, having again changed location, reached back for a reloaded rifle, only to be disappointed. Cursing, he glanced around for Forrest. That individual was extracting the ramrod from his rifle barrel and hadn't yet followed on.

'Get over here, you tardy son of a bitch,' he barked. 'I can't do this all on my lonesome!'

Forrest glared at his belligerent companion with real anger. His left arm was aching something terrible and he was heartily sick of being ordered about. 'Leave me be, you God-damn pus weasel!' he yelled back. 'I'm giving it my best.'

So saying, and with his blood well and truly up, he carelessly clambered to his feet and made a dash for it. The irate private had covered maybe three yards when the first of two projectiles struck him. The first one slammed into his right breast, causing him to slew sideways. Then, because the unrestrained bow had shifted with the current, he found himself bizarrely staring directly at his executioners on the bank. With remarkable accuracy, the second ball struck him full on between the eyes, before bloodily removing the back of his skull.

As Metford witnessed his crony tumble to the deck, a red mist seemed to rise before his eyes. He had never really thought of the other man as his friend, because such a concept was unfamiliar to him. Yet now that Rab was irrevocably gone, he was assailed by a tremendous feeling of loss . . . and rage. Those bastard rebs were going to pay for this!

Staying low, he scurried over to his blood-soaked comrade and seized the loaded rifle. Then, with a long gun in each hand, he made for the steps leading to the deck below.

'Where the hell are you going, soldier?' Paulding demanded.

Metford's response was uncompromising, and completely lacking in deference. 'You get this tub moving, while I kill me some Johnny Rebs!' And then, before the vessel's captain had time to remonstrate, he was gone.

Another young officer below stared in amazement at the powder-burned infantryman stalking across his gun deck. 'What the devil do you want?' he challenged. Just like his leader, the response was not what he had expected.

'Get those poxy guns run out,' Metford ordered. The strangely manic gleam in his eyes was decidedly disconcerting.

Nevertheless, the officer shook his head. 'Don't be ridiculous. Those bastards'll just pick off my men again. Get off my deck, now!'

Amazingly, the muzzle of one of the Springfields drifted towards his face. The threat was unmistakable. 'I'm here to see they don't . . . at your captain's command,' the soldier rasped. 'Now get those big guns run out, or I might just have to pop a cap on you.'

The other man's eyes widened like saucers, as it occurred to him that this apparition appeared crazy enough to do just that. Then one of his ratings close by called out, 'She's got movement aft now, Lieutenant. Happen we might be able to place some shot on those bastards in the trees . . . if they're not free to move about.'

The officer pondered for a moment, all the while conscious of the gaping muzzle before him. 'Oh, very well. Load the port guns with grape,' he tersely ordered, 'and then run them out.' To Metford he added, 'You'd best pick your spot. And God help you if this doesn't answer!'

The private grinned wolfishly before turning away. Squatting next to a sloping gun port, he cocked a rifle and waited. At his side was a massive smooth-bore Dahlgren. 'You be sure an' tell me when you're fixing to fire this beast,' he muttered to the gun captain.

Then, with an ominous creaking, the armoured barriers began to rise outwards and upwards, allow-ing light to flood the cramped deck. Metford immediately thrust his rifle into the gap and drew a bead on one of the rebels. His aim was true, and the butternut grey figure pitched forwards into the Tennessee with a strangled cry. Quickly switching weapons, the Union man sought out another target. His deadly presence had obviously distracted the Confederates, because despite some hurried sniping, not a single sailor was hit.

Then the gunnery officer yelled out, 'Run out the port battery,' and Metford hastily backed off.

One of the ratings considerately gestured for him to cover his ears, which he did, but nevertheless the resulting broadside was mind-numbing in its inten-sity. The soldier had, of course, experienced artillery discharging in the open, but nothing could have pre-pared him for its effects in an enclosed space. His skull felt as if it must surely split under the shockwave that swept the deck. The prospect of enduring more such blasts filled him with dismay.

'Holy shit,' he mumbled. Or maybe he shouted. He couldn't really tell.

With his senses reeling, he staggered over to the gun port. Initially all he could see was smoke. Then it cleared on the wind, and he was able to witness the devastation wrought by four naval guns loaded with grape. Because this time they had been trained in the right direction, on men who had lost freedom of movement. Shredded oaks were literally splashed with blood. Dismembered corpses lay amongst the trees, and although Metford had his rifle ready, there was no longer anything worth shooting at.

Then from the rear of the boat there came a churning sound as the single paddle wheel returned to life. Surprisingly to the soldier, the vessel initially seemed to be going backwards, as its captain sought to free the anchor. This action was followed by a deal of shouting and the sound of tramping feet, until abruptly the direction was reversed and the USS *Pittsburgh* recommenced its journey downriver.

Metford gently lowered the hammer on his Springfield, and as the lieutenant ordered, 'Close the gun ports,' the reluctant soldier smiled grimly. Thank the Lord he wouldn't have to endure another broadside!

As Jason Metford returned to the upper deck, he had no idea what the future held for him. With the gunboat no longer under threat, it seemed very likely that his insubordination would result in some form of retribution. And it appeared that he wouldn't have long to wait.

'You there,' Lieutenant Paulding bellowed across the deck. 'Present yourself!'

Still carrying two rifles, the infantryman did just that. What happened next came as a mighty big surprise, because unbelievably the officer thrust out his right hand. 'You are without doubt a thoroughly insubordinate and rude fellow. . . but you have unquestionably saved the lives of many of my crew, and maybe even this vessel. I don't know why Captain Reynolds took agin you, and I don't care. As far as I'm concerned you have more than earned my gratitude, and your passage to Fort Donelson.'

Such fulsome praise was, of course, a double-edged sword, because the last thing Metford desired was to rejoin Grant's army. Then again, a well of good feeling might just come in useful if that God-damned marshal ever showed up again!

Paulding hadn't quite finished. 'It was a shame about your friend.'

Metford shrugged. 'He had it coming, I guess.' His somewhat shallow remorse suddenly reminded him that he hadn't yet checked Forrest's pockets for specie. Although rarely prone to any deep contemplation, it did then occur to him that he was now the sole remaining fugitive.

CHAPTER EIGHT

The USS *Tyler* slowed to a crawl so that its captain and passengers could scrutinize the carnage on the river-bank. 'Looks to have been quite a set-to,' Frank Pootes remarked. 'How's about letting me take a look-see, Lieutenant?'

The gunboat's young commander regarded him dubiously. Although far from sure as to the extent of a federal marshal's authority on a naval vessel in time of war, one thing he did know was that his small crew wasn't equipped to get embroiled in a skirmish on land. And whilst inordinately proud of his first command, the officer was very aware that the position of its side wheels made it vulnerable to flanking fire. That, and the fact that his boat possessed no armour plate at all, meant that he wasn't ever keen on getting too close to the bank. He also couldn't fathom the point of such a request. 'What if there's still some live ones hidden in the trees?' he finally asked.

Pootes' lop-sided smile displayed rather more confidence than he actually felt. 'This fine repeater will

103

guarantee our scalps,' he replied, levering a cartridge into the Henry's breech.

The naval officer regarded him askance. 'You're asking a lot, Marshal.'

'What I'm *asking* is to be rowed ashore to view the evidence. That's the limit of your involvement.'

'Evidence of what?' the other man demanded incredulously. 'Hopefully there's just a mess of dead bodies over there!'

Pootes sighed impatiently. He was getting tired of having to continually explain himself to the God-damn military. 'That my fugitive was somehow involved. Because, believe it or not, catching him is the only reason I'm taking this purdy boat ride.'

Something in his voice told the lieutenant that it might be best just to humour this lawman. And in any case he supposed it might be useful to identify enemy casualties and any unit that they were from. 'Very well,' he finally responded. 'We'll reverse up the river a-piece, so that the current can carry your rowboat inshore. Then we'll move on downriver, so that you can easily rejoin us. That way, if anyone seeks to do you harm, at least you'll have some speed. How's that suit, Marshal?'

'Oh, that'll do just dandy,' came the caustic response.

As the two men cautiously clambered out of the small boat and up on to the riverbank, they gazed around in horror at the devastation wrought by the *Pittsburgh*'s broadside. Body parts were strewn grotesquely amongst the trees, so that it was barely possible to make out how many men had been involved. Although no strangers to bloody violence, both of them struggled against the bile rising in their throats. One of the two ratings who had rowed them ashore crossed himself and muttered, 'Holy shit! Will you look at that!' All of a sudden they had no desire to poke about amongst the gruesome detritus, orders or not. Even the possibility of plunder no longer held any charms.

And yet, not all the cadavers had been torn to pieces. The army sergeant came across one that was almost unmarked . . . at least at the front. He only had to glance at the neat entry hole between the sightless eyes. 'Whatever else dished out all these hard knocks, this man was kilt by a Minie ball, an' no mistake.'

Pootes nodded. 'An' since yours is the only Springfield I've seen on the *Tyler*, I reckon the same might be true of the *Pittsburgh*. All of which means this was likely done by our man. And another thing. These folks are not long dead, so we are catching up with him.' His eyes unwillingly strayed to the carnage around him and he swallowed. 'Let's get the hell out of here, Sergeant. Whatever contrary opinions they held, these were still fellow Americans, and all this just makes me sick.'

It was as Rhodes turned to the boat that he glimpsed a rifle muzzle poking out of the undergrowth. His heart leapt with shock, until he realized that there was no one behind it. Hurrying over, he

105

seized hold of the Enfield and remarked, 'This'll give the lieutenant something to show for stopping here: yet another rifle made by the "John Bulls" and sold for profit to kill our countrymen with.' He paused as a further thought struck him. 'You know, Marshal, God willing, we could catch up with the powder-marked bastard before Cairo.'

Which just went to prove that Sam Rhodes possessed far more optimism than sense, because he ought to have known that in love and war nothing ever happens as it should. But then again, everybody deserves a little luck sometimes!

Fort Donelson was certain to present a far tougher challenge to Grant's forces than had Fort Henry. Constructed on the west bank of the Cumberland to cover a bend in the river, it was intended to control access into Tennessee, and then on into the very heart of the Confederacy. Situated on high ground, there were also extensive entrenchments manned by recently arrived reinforcements to command the land approaches. Being mostly piled earth, the structure shared no similarity with the ubiquitous timber stockades that had long been a feature of the frontier.

As well as a variety of ancient and modern ordnance, including two 32-pounders, the fort boasted a simply monstrous 128-pounder cannon. Not even Foote's ironclads, if they were foolish enough to get within range, could withstand solid shot from such a behemoth. And knowing that a fight was surely coming, Confederate engineers had been improving the defences by building additional breastworks and digging rifle pits. Yet it was a sad fact that such apparent strength could be illusory.

Brigadier General Gideon Johnson Pillow gazed down at the sweating enlisted men as they wielded their makeshift entrenching tools. As everywhere in the embattled Confederacy, there was always a shortage of equipment. He was well aware that it was only the knowledge of his brooding presence that brought forth such effort. And in truth, the general couldn't blame them, because he knew that up against the combined might of Grant's well-supplied army *and* navy the fortress's days were definitely numbered. Despite its positioning and impressive firepower, Fort Donelson couldn't hope to survive a sustained assault by both land and river. Fort Henry's swiftly reached fate had surely confirmed that. Yet it was Pillow's sworn duty to hold back the Union advance for as long as possible, and that was just what he intended to do.

Sensing movement at his side, the fort's recently appointed commander turned to find the hard, rangy features of yet another of the general officers that he had been saddled with. Yet unlike the others, who were mostly political appointees, this one bore the unmistakably chill demeanour of a born killer. Nathan Bedford Forrest was a self-made plantation owner, former slave trader and so-called 'Southern gentleman', who had rapidly gained a reputation for ruthless, brutal efficiency and the uncanny ability to 'use' a piece of ground to his advantage. He presently commanded an under-strength brigade of cavalry, and had already delayed for a whole day the advance of Union troops by effectively skirmishing with them until ordered back to Fort Donelson. He made no secret of the fact that he chafed under the restrictions of garrison duty . . . as he was about to confirm.

'So there's no misremembering, I speak plain and to your face,' Forrest rasped, 'When those damned Yankees finally get here and invest these fortifications, *as they will*, I intend to lead my men out of this death trap and take the fight to the enemy. With or without your permission.'

As he formulated a response, Pillow endeavoured to match the other man's piercing stare. Yet although he had served with some distinction in the Mexican War, he found himself disconcerted by Forrest's magnetic aura of raw power and determination. 'Don't over-reach yourself, General,' he finally managed. 'You have been placed under my command until I say otherwise. If you attempt to leave without my permission I will have you arrested.' Such confrontational words were barely out of his mouth before he regretted them.

Stepping almost nose-to-nose in front of his commanding officer, a manic gleam came to Forrest's habitually wintry eyes. Thin lips momentarily compressed within his devilishly contoured beard. Then, with his right hand caressing the handmade leather holster containing a massive LeMat revolver, he dramatically reaffirmed his position.

'If I should see fit to take *my* brigade out of *your* fort, there is nothing on this earth that will prevent me . . . and you would do well to remember that. *And,* if I manage to hit the Yankees in their flanks and put a real scare into them, you might even have cause to thank me. So count your blessings and don't attempt to make a mortal enemy of me, General *Pillow*!'

Having said his piece, the cavalry commander abruptly turned and strode away, leaving Pillow to mull over the short but bruising encounter. He hadn't missed the emphasis of his somewhat less-than-warlike surname, and it did just occur to him that whilst Ulysses Grant was undoubtedly his enemy, and the possessor of far more resources, Nathan Forrest was much the more terrifying!

Since the USS *Tyler* was not only less prone to engine troubles than the *Pittsburgh,* but also much faster due to its lack of heavy armour plating, the former caught up with the latter that same afternoon. The Union depot at Cairo was still some miles off, which meant that the lawman was more than a little hopeful of finding his fugitives on board. Yet he would have to wait a little longer, because unsurprisingly, as they came level, the wooden gunboat's commanding officer couldn't resist tossing a few ribald remarks across to his opposite number.

'Would it help if we were to send over a tow line?' was one of his more helpful offerings. With the sergeant at his side, Frank Pootes waited impatiently until the lieutenant had finished with his juvenile banter before seizing his opportunity.

'I am a Deputy United States Marshal, working out of Frankfort, Kentucky. Do you have two Union soldiers aboard?' the marshal hollered across. His Henry was cocked and ready, but held out of sight behind the gunwale.

The swift and surprising response was an emphatic 'No', which in itself was not untrue, because Rab Forrest, unsurprisingly no relation to the Confederate general, had been consigned to the bottom of the river many miles back. What was perhaps astonishing was that a naval officer would consider lying for a lowly private soldier, but then this one *had* just helped to save his precious vessel.

Shaking his head in disbelief, the lawman tried again. 'How can that be? Captain Reynolds informed me that he placed them under your command.'

'That was then and this is now,' came the uncompromising reply. 'We were attacked by rebels upriver a piece, and both men were shot dead defending this boat.'

'Then I need to see the bodies,' Pootes retorted testily.

'So get to swimming,' Paulding barked back before turning away. The distinctly unsatisfactory conversation was apparently over.

The marshal blinked in disbelief before glancing at Rhodes. 'What do you make of that, Sergeant?'

The other man shrugged his broad shoulders. 'Ain't for me to gainsay an officer . . . but happen you were to press me, I'd say it was a crock of shit!'

Pootes turned to the Tyler's captain. 'Can you get me over to that boat?'

It was the lieutenant's turn to register disbelief. After vigorously shaking his head, he replied, 'Unless he chooses to stop, a rowing boat isn't fast enough, and I can't risk damaging the side paddles by getting too close.'

'God damn it all to hell!' the lawman exclaimed. 'There *must* be something we can do.' For long moments he pondered the situation before coming to a decision. Focusing all his attention on the young officer, he barked, 'What's your name, son? 'Cause it sure ain't just *Lieutenant*.'

Although clearly startled at being addressed in such a fashion on the deck of his own vessel, the ruddy-faced sailor answered gamely enough. 'Collier. John Collier. And I ain't your son, so if you want considerations from me you'd best mind your tongue on this boat!'

Amazingly, the marshal suddenly favoured him with a broad smile. 'Well said, John Collier. I like a man with grit.' He paused to choose his next words carefully. 'Since you can't get me on to that boat, I need you to stick with it like a fly on shit. If our fugitives are still on it, and I reckon they are, then we can't give them the chance to skedaddle.'

Despite the fraught circumstances, Sergeant Rhodes sniggered. 'Ha! *Grit* and *shit*. You ought to be a poet, Marshal.'

Collier regarded his passengers askance. 'I'm

under orders from Flag Officer Foote to proceed to Fort Donelson, and I ain't disobeying him for you or anyone else.'

The lawman sighed and gestured over at the *Pittsburgh*. 'And where's he bound for?'

Collier's brow furrowed. 'The same place, of course.'

Pootes spread his hands wide, as though in supplication. 'So what's the problem? All I'm asking is that you keep pace with your fellow officer until he pulls in somewhere. Where's the harm in that? Eh, eh?'

The lieutenant couldn't think of a good answer to that, so he changed tack slightly. 'You must want these men very badly. Mind telling me why?'

As on every occasion that he disclosed his story, the lawman's features grew hard and grim. 'One or both of them done raped my niece to death up in Kentucky. It had nothing to do with the war against the south. They're just evil characters, through and through.'

Although now sadly used to warfare, Collier was noticeably shocked. 'By Christ! I reckon that explains everything and then some. But why didn't you tell Paulding?'

Pootes didn't even have to think about that one. 'Because if those bastards *are* still on his boat, then he's already lied once. The question is, why?'

Leonard Paulding glanced surreptitiously over at the USS *Tyler* and swore under his breath. Despite its greater speed, the wooden gunboat was keeping station on his starboard side. It was obvious that the federal marshal, whoever he was, had convinced Collier to stay close. Anger flared within him at the implication that he was now under surveillance by a fellow officer. And yet with anger came doubt. Doubt at his lack of sense in having lied for an enlisted man about whom he knew nothing.

That powder-marked individual was currently skulking out of sight on the gun deck, and Paulding briefly pondered over whether to demand a reason for what was obviously a determined pursuit by a lawman. Then he realized that there was little point. Because of that one well-meaning lie, Paulding was now committed to maintaining the fiction that Private Metford was dead. And that appalling state of affairs would have to continue until he either actually became deceased in reality, or was able to leave the *Pittsburgh* undetected. Which, with the *Tyler* shadowing their every move, meant that the infantryman was likely to be on board until they attacked Fort Donelson. At that point there would likely be enough concerted mayhem to affect the man's disappearance. But how he would square the whole business with his crew was another matter entirely!

CHAPTER NINE

Brigadier General Gideon Pillow peered anxiously downriver through a battered drawtube spyglass that somehow seemed to belong to another age. In the early morning light he could just discern plumes of smoke rising up over the treetops that bordered the Cumberland River. They informed him that his men would soon be fighting to defend the fort, rather than labouring to strengthen it. With a sinking heart he next searched intently, but in vain, for any signs of Grant's land forces, because if the gunboats were on their way, then so must be that 'up and coming' general. Then Fort Donelson's commander recalled the reports from some of Fort Henry's escapees, that Foote's ironclads had attacked first in the hope of smashing the defences before the Union troops had to be committed. Since it had worked there, it made sense to assume that the same tactics would be attempted again.

Although he had no illusions as to his long-term chances of success, Pillow was very conscious of the fact that Albert Sidney Johnston, currently the

Confederacy's foremost general, had personally appointed him to his position. Therefore he had no choice other than to do everything in his power to defend the fortress. Sighing, he lowered the spyglass and turned away. The bearded, good-looking general supposed that he ought to order the 'stand-to', but he was unaccountably reluctant. Perhaps, since he was no stranger to warfare, it was because he knew all too well just what would follow.

'The enemy approaches. Assemble the men,' he finally bellowed at one of his officers. That impossibly young individual, still keen and immaculate in his grey uniform with its highly polished accoutrements, literally jumped to attention before rapidly complying. It appeared that the time for contemplation was over. The killing season had resumed!

'Fire!'

With a deafening, ragged crash that shook the USS *Tyler* to its very keel, half of the gunboat's main armament discharged. Blasts of flame and acrid smoke erupted out of the gaping muzzles and on across the Cumberland River, effectively announcing to the Confedcracy that another siege had begun. And as if all that wasn't enough, the same occurred on the six accompanying vessels. The combination of noise and shock was indescribable. Yet this was only the first of many volleys that were intended to be unleashed on the distant fort.

Although his ears rang painfully from the appalling detonations, Frank Pootes didn't allow the discomfort to distract him from his primary task. Consequently, his attention remained mostly on the *Pittsburgh*, because he knew full well that his fugitives might decide to take advantage of the clouds of smoke. Beside him on deck, Sergeant Rhodes waited patiently for a brief interlude in the firing.

'You ever seen the like of this before?' he finally managed, his expression surprisingly sympathetic.

Without taking his eyes off the other boat, Pootes grunted and replied, 'I served in the Mexican War under old "rough and ready" Zachary Taylor, so it ain't all new to me. But I'll allow I never got this close to any big guns.'

As if to emphasize that, another broadside thundered out, and despite his studied nonchalance, Rhodes winced with the blast and observed: 'It sure is something to behold!'

That sentiment was shared by Flag Officer Andrew Hull Foote as he observed the fall of shot from his flagship nearby. With the *Cincinnati* under repair, he had transferred his flag to the USS *St Louis*, and it was from this ironclad that he was leading the naval assault on Fort Donelson. And unfortunately for the men under his command, his natural impatience was about to get them all into a whole heap of trouble.

By keeping his flotilla at a distance, he was able to inflict damage on the fort without receiving any in return. *But*, at Fort Henry his boats had got in close, successfully finishing the bloody business quickly, and he was strongly minded to repeat the manoeuvre.

Abruptly coming to a decision, he gave orders for all craft to cease fire and immediately resume their advance upriver, full steam ahead.

Jason Metford cursed fluently under his breath. With the *Pittsburgh* immobile and all hands occupied in fighting the boat, he had agreed with himself that it was time to take advantage of the thick smoke and leave the God-damn navy to their own devices. By cutting loose one of the small boats, he reckoned that he could be off downriver before anyone had the chance to stop him – if indeed they would even bother trying. And if the poxy law dog *was* still watching out for him, there would be little that cockchafer could do other than belatedly follow on in a similar craft, because there was no way in hell any gunboat was going to break off the fight to give chase. That was how he saw it, anyhu. But then, quite abruptly, the big guns ceased firing and all seven vessels got under way again. There really was no justice!

General Pillow stared through his spyglass in disbelief at the fast-approaching Union flotilla. Seven gunboats, four of them armoured. Even from a considerable distance, some of their modern, rifled cannon had inflicted a frightening amount of death and destruction on his command. The shattered bodies of the dead and dying lay around him to prove it. And yet here they were, unnecessarily steaming to close quarters, where his big smoothbores could do even an ironclad some real harm. The general couldn't believe his good fortune. Here was his chance to maybe make a name for himself, and in so doing render irrelevant Nathan Forrest's annoying insistence on fighting the enemy independently. Because when it came to bolstering authority, there was nothing more effective than success.

'Fire only on my command,' he bellowed down to the nearest gun emplacements. Such was his excitement that he had dispensed with the accepted formality of calmly relaying orders through a junior officer. And still the enemy craft drew nearer. From then on the tension within him grew until his stomach felt as though it was in knots. 'Come on, come on,' he muttered feverishly. 'Just a bit closer.'

In an attempt to diffuse his anxiety, he concentrated his attention on each individual ironclad. He noted their dark, squat ugliness and somehow sinister lines. They completely lacked the grace and style of a traditional sailing ship, but then he supposed that that was the inevitable price of progress. Because, like it or not, steam power had changed everything. Then the seven vessels began to turn, to allow their varied selection of guns to bear, and he knew it was time.

'Fire at will,' Pillow hollered, and almost immediately Fort Donelson's cannon crashed out their defiance. Dominating the stunning discharge was the awesome roar of the 128-pounder, known proudly by its extensive gun crew as 'the smasher'. Its massive piece of solid shot hit only water, but close enough to one of the ironclads to drench its crew. Next time it would surely do better.

'Send a general signal to lower elevation, God damn it,' Flag Officer Foote commanded angrily amidst the din of battle. To his certain knowledge, since reaching point blank range, barely any of the flotilla's shot had done any damage, which was plainly ridiculous against such a sizeable target. Then, from the environs of the rebel fort, the 'smasher' fired again, and the dreadful sound of rending metal came to him across the river. 'What the devil have they got in there?' he queried, before glancing anxiously over at the USS *Pittsburgh*.

That particular gunboat appeared to have sustained a direct hit by something that had cleaved its armour like a knife through butter. Even through the fog of war, the naval commander could make out the dreadfully mutilated and blood-soaked bodies of some of its crew. It was at that moment that the first inklings of doubt came to him over his decision to repeat the tactics used at Fort Henry. But by then, of course, it was far too late.

Jason Metford viewed the sheer mayhem around him with real alarm. He knew what it was like to stand in a line of infantry and take incoming fire, but this was something else entirely. He hadn't actually seen the piece of shot that had struck the *Pittsburgh*, but the shock of it had literally knocked him off his feet. So now he lay at the rear of the single gun deck listening to the myriad screams coming from above. The terrified, but so far unharmed gun crews were frantically working to return fire when a bellowed command reached their muffled ears.

'Order from the flag. Depress your barrels!'

Cursing, harassed sailors began to turn the screws that altered their guns' elevation. All of which took time, which they were about to run out of. Because before those near the front of the deck could deliver another broadside, something struck the iron plate armour just above their gun ports like a freight train and kept on coming. Ploughing on through the boat's timbers, the massive piece of shot hit a gun carriage and sent it spinning like a skittle. That, combined with jagged splinters from the shattered oak, meant the resulting carnage was simply terrible to behold.

Luckless victims were crushed, torn or skewered like so many insects. With every surface splashed with blood, fresh screams rang out to compete with those from above. The runaway gun miraculously came to a halt mere inches from Metford, and only because its muzzle got wedged into a section of broken decking.

'The hell with this!' he mumbled. Having naively assumed that ironclads were proof against enemy fire, the harsh reality had come as a shock. Getting shakily to his feet, he grabbed both Springfields, slung one over each shoulder and headed for the stairway. His progress was slowed by the blood and gore that coated the deck, but finally he made it. Unsurprisingly, no one had made any attempt to stop him. Even as he mounted the stairs it occurred to him that the damned law dog was very probably out there on the *Tyler*, watching and waiting, but there could be no help for it. If he remained where he was he would like as not get torn to pieces by splinters when the next massive chunk of solid shot arrived.

The *Pittsburgh*'s upper deck proved to be no less gruesome. Part of the starboard bulwark had been destroyed, and there were several dead and wounded with horrific injuries. Lieutenant Paulding was fully occupied in the wheelhouse, and so Metford padded over to the stern hoping to find a rowing boat that he might cut loose. Sadly, all required the use of block and tackle for them to be winched over the side, which was hopelessly beyond the scope of a lone fugitive. Cursing, he turned away looking for anything to aid his departure, and his glance happened to fall on the USS *Tyler* coming up at the rear. Staring directly at him were two men: one a civilian and the other wearing an army uniform similar to his own.

'Oh shit!' he exclaimed.

'Got you, you bastard!' Frank Pootes cried out. 'D'you see him?'

'Oh, I see him all right,' Sam Rhodes responded. 'Question is, what do we do about it?' The thought of actually shooting at the USS *Pittsburgh* would never have occurred to him.

The lawman's answer to that was to immediately tuck the Henry into his shoulder and open fire. Under normal circumstances, and at such range, his first shot would have done the job. Unfortunately for him, there was nothing normal about any of it, least of all the swaying deck beneath his boots. And so the first and second bullets merely ricocheted off armour plate, thereby proving that the iron could at least stop something.

'God damn it all to hell, can't you keep this boat still?' Pootes yelled angrily at the wheelhouse. But of course, no one was listening to such a patently ridiculous demand. And then, even as he levered in a fresh cartridge, his prey was on the move. The blue-clad soldier shrugged off one of the rifles, rearranged the other across his back, and then simply vaulted over the side.

'Don't even think about following him,' Rhodes hotly remarked. 'I don't swim so good.'

The marshal glared at him in exasperation for a moment before turning away to search out the boat's commander. 'Collier,' he hollered. 'If you want to help us catch that murdering rapist, get one of your rowing boats in the water. They were on the *Pittsburgh*, or at least one of them was, and now he's swimming for the riverbank.'

Not for the first time, the young officer stared at him askance. 'For Christ's sake, Marshal. We're in the middle of a battle here!' That was a slight exaggeration, because as yet no enemy shot had come anywhere near the *Tyler*. It seemed that the Confederates were first concentrating their efforts against the supposedly more dangerous ironclads.

'All I want is one little boat,' Pootes persisted.

'Then you're rid of us for good. That's got to be a fair exchange.'

The gunboat shook as yet another salvo was unleashed against the rebel positions, but John Collier barely noticed. 'Oh, very well.' He issued the relevant order to a petty officer, and a boat was let down on to the Cumberland; as it was being lowered he put one question to the lawman: 'Is all this worth it? After all, he is still a soldier in the Union army, you know. And if you come up against any Johnny Rebs out there, you could get into all kinds of trouble.'

As Pootes headed for the gunwale, his answer was unequivocal. 'I don't give a rat's ass what army he's in or who he is. He's answerable for what he did to my niece. And that sure as hell didn't have anything to do with this damned war.' And with that, he seized hold of a rope as though his life depended upon it, and tentatively swung a leg over the side. 'I'm obliged to you, Lieutenant Collier,' he remarked, before lowering himself over the side. 'Are you coming, Sergeant?'

Even though he was no longer required to swim anywhere, Rhodes was still reluctant to depart the larger vessel in the middle of a river. 'I'm a soldier, not a sailor,' he protested.

The voice from below was unyielding. 'Just get in the damn boat!'

The instant Private Metford hit the river, he knew that he was in big trouble. . . and not from any

higher power. Although not in one of the high lati-
tudes, it was still winter, and the water was absolutely
God-damn freezing. The dreadful shock was such
that he thought his heart must surely stop. Then the
combined weight of his clothing and the heavy rifle
on his back immediately began to drag him down,
and for a brief moment he was seized by raw panic.
With icy liquid invading every orifice, all thoughts of
the enemy or even escaping the tarnal law dog left
him. And where he might end up was also abruptly
irrelevant, because just surviving the Cumberland
was suddenly all that mattered.

As he struggled to the surface, kicking and splut-
tering, the current drew him back downriver, and he
made no attempt to resist it. In fact, the numbing
cold was so intense that he could quite easily have
succumbed to it, except that he had never been a
quitter. And so he frantically thrashed about, completely oblivious to the dreadful rending crash
behind him, as another lump of solid shot struck the
Pittsburgh. Drawing on all his reserves of energy, he
struck out for the nearest bank, which just happened
to be the side occupied by Fort Donelson.

His frantic, lone battle against the forces of nature
seemed to take forever, although in reality it was only
a few minutes. With the Springfield digging painfully
into his back, he ploughed on through the seemingly
freezing water until abruptly his boots struck solid
ground. Contact with the riverbed brought a surge of
hope, but he wasn't in the clear yet. Desperately
trying to control his rapid breathing, Metford finally

and very gratefully staggered into the shallows and then up on to the bank. Quite unbelievably he had survived . . . the river!

Without any warning, an inert stone suddenly leapt into the air barely inches from his head. The single gunshot had been engulfed by the all-pervading din of battle, but even that couldn't completely overwhelm the harsh voice that rang out over the water.

'Stand fast, you cockchafer!'

The sodden fugitive didn't need to look to know who was trying to kill him. Staggering to his feet, he fled into the screen of trees without a backward glance.

'Sweet Jesus!' Pootes cried out in bitter frustration as he levered in another cartridge. He normally hit what he aimed at, and longed to be back on solid ground. 'I've had a bellyful of this swaying shit. Can't you row any faster?'

In truth, Sam Rhodes, having once got into a rhythm, was putting everything into his task, and they were fast closing on the tree-lined bank. It was not his fault that their prey had already slipped out of sight.

As the small boat finally grounded in the shallows, Pootes leapt out, his repeater at the ready. He knew that after its immersion, their foe's muzzle-loading Springfield would be useless, but he had already seen what that man was capable of with a blade. Behind him, the sergeant was panting heavily from the unaccustomed form of exercise, and took his own sweet time disembarking.

'What would you have me do with the boat?' he finally gasped.

Grateful to be back on terra firma, Pootes would happily have torched it, but resisted such a childish impulse. 'Best pull it ashore,' he reluctantly ordered. 'Just in case.'

As though adding value to that remark, the fearful violence on and around the river seemed to reach new heights. And on a brief scrutiny it appeared as though the Union gunboats were getting the worst of it. Unfortunately, the USS *Tyler* looked to have taken a direct hit and was listing badly.

'God damn it,' Rhodes exclaimed bitterly. 'That shouldn't ought to have happened.' But then, with a conscious effort, he put the whole business out of his mind. Because, after all, he was neither in the navy nor even in Tennessee to fight Confederates any more . . . apparently. Although if his temporary leader wasn't careful that could change.

Glancing around, the lawman quickly spotted foliage that had been recently trampled by someone in a hurry. 'This way,' he remarked, and immediately set off like a bloodhound with a fresh scent.

Trembling violently with cold, Metford recognized that his best chance of warming himself up *and* avoiding a bullet was to keep moving. With his rifle and the contents of his cartridge pouch rendered unusable by river water, he found himself instinctively heading towards the enemy fortifications, on the basis that if all else failed he could always approach the rebels as a deserter. Because, whilst he had no interest in fighting to preserve slavery, returning to the Union army with the lawman hot on his heels was out of the question.

A natural desire to remain hidden meant that he had to keep the river close, because once away from the bank the trees were replaced by open farmland. Squelching along in his army issue boots and saturated uniform, Metford felt his spirits sinking. How had it all come to this? It was altogether the fault of that winsome bitch up in Kentucky, he decided. Cursing fluently, he ground to a halt next to a large oak tree. The chaffing of the Springfield across his wet back had grown intolerable. Come what may, he would have to shift it.

The abrupt agony in his right ear sent him reeling into cover behind the oak, which is where he should have been in the first place. With blood pouring from his mutilated appendage, he desperately tried to locate his assailant. Then a chunk of bark flew from the tree, but such was the noise of battle he still didn't hear the shot. And up against that poxy repeating rifle there would doubtless be plenty more to come, unless they chose to close in on him. Either way, there wasn't a damn thing he could do about it!

The totally unexpected flurry of gunshots came from the direction of the fort. They had to have been very close to be heard, but amazingly they didn't seem to be aimed at him. And then the sound of

thrumming hoof beats joined in. Dazed by the excru-
ciating pain from his wound, Metford peered over at
the grey-coated horsemen who had seemingly
appeared out of nowhere, and were now exchanging
hot lead with his two pursuers. The rapid rate of fire
from the marshal must have surprised them, because
rather than ride him down, the Confederate cavalry
instead swung off towards the injured private.
Strangely, considering his dire straits, he couldn't
help thinking that they appeared born to the saddle.
Then one of them pointed a British-made Adams
revolver directly at his head and smiled.

'Rot in hell, Yankee!'

CHAPTER TEN

Brigadier General Nathan Bedford Forrest briefly settled his hard eyes on the bedraggled specimen of Union manhood swaying slightly before him. Blood-soaked and bizarrely dripping river water, the manacled prisoner pathetically held his head to one side, as though seeking relief for what precious little remained of his right ear. Most of the flesh had been shot away, and the pain must have been quite fright-ful – which was only right and proper, since these damn Yankees had no business invading Tennessee in the first place.

The cavalry detachment had reported back to Forrest within the extensive confines of Fort Donelson. The only thing particularly puzzling the general was why this miserable wretch still lived. But, well aware of Captain Le Favre's soldierly qualities, he knew that there had to be a good reason for the captive's continued existence.

'Why is this sack of shit still drawing breath?' the general demanded. Unlike a lot of southern officers, he had no time for flowery speech or false gentility. His hard beginnings had imbued him with an exceptionally harsh view of the conflict. 'War means fighting. And fighting means killing!' was something he never tired of expounding.

'My sergeant was about to pop a cap on the Yankee . . . until I stopped him,' the captain replied.

Forrest's jet-black eyebrows rose. His question still hadn't been answered. 'For why?'

'He was being pursued by both a Union sergeant, and a civilian with one of those new-fangled repeating rifles that they load on a Sunday and shoot all week. What I wouldn't give for a crate of those. Anyhu, they seemed awful keen to get him, 'cause it was one of them that shot his ear off. So we gave them a wide berth and took this cuss with us.'

The general grunted. 'Seems like a lot of fuss for a lowly private, even a deserter.' He abruptly closed in on Metford, who gazed at his grim visage with very real fear. 'What's your name, soldier?'

Despite his parlous situation, the wounded man couldn't resist a little bravado. 'I got lots of names, your honour. One each time I join a regiment for bounty.'

The powerful backhand slap took the prisoner completely by surprise and rocked him back on his heels. Fresh blood flowed from a mashed lip where Forrest's leather gauntlet had caught him.

'Don't sass me, boy,' the Confederate snarled, seizing the grip of his sabre. 'Or I'll gut you like a fish!' With menace apparently emanating from every pore, his piercing eyes bored into those of his victim.

When it came to self-preservation, Jason Metford was not slow on the uptake. And the pitiless gaze that seemingly penetrated his very soul hinted that he would only get the one chance to stake his claim on survival. So whatever story he concocted would have to be pretty damn good. And just when he needed it most, a doozy of an idea popped into his tormented skull.

'My given name's Jason. But everyone as wants to, calls me Jase,' he blurted out, before rapidly moving on to something more informative. 'The bastard with the Henry rifle is a Pinkerton.'

There was a flicker of recognition on Forrest's forbidding features. Certainly enough to give Metford a glimmer of hope. Through their spies in Washington, the Confederate government had learned of the Pinkerton Detective Agency's activities. Established twelve years earlier by its namesake, Allan Pinkerton, it currently specialized in providing information to the Union army on the size and disposition of the South's forces. The fact that it often over-estimated these was not generally realized, at least certainly not by the North.

Forrest professionally scrutinized the private's grisly wound, and rightly concluded that the bullet had definitely been intended to kill, because in the heat of the action nobody taking the shot could have deliberately chosen the amount of damage to inflict.

'So even if you were a deserter, why would a

Pinkerton agent try his damnedest to kill *you*, a mere private?'

Metford recognized that the time had come for him to be at his most inventive, with his life depending on the outcome. 'Well, I'll tell you, General, sir,' he drawled. 'A couple of nights past, I just happened to find myself mighty close by Grant's tent. He's the big cheese in these parts. The sentry had sloped off for a piss, an' I guess I just got curious as to what his high-up kind get to jawing about. Anyhu, there was him an' another general, old Smith I think. They was talking about their plans after they take this place. Right informative they were too, if you get my drift.' So saying, he winked conspiratorially at the cavalry general. 'But then the tarnal sentry came back, an' I had to hightail it. Shame was, he spotted me. An' that's the which of why that Pinkerton tried to part my hair with a bullet. The bastards must have got to thinking that I'd heard too much.'

Forrest stared at him with ill-concealed contempt. 'And can you recall all that you overheard?'

Realizing that he had definitely attracted the other man's interest, Metford retorted with surprising boldness: 'I might be something you'd wipe off your boot, General, but I ain't entirely stupid.'

Before he could respond, Forrest was forestalled by an outbreak of firing on the landward approaches to the fort.

'Union skirmishers, sir,' one of his officers announced from a nearby breastwork. 'And there's massed ranks of infantry close behind. Looks like they mean business.'

The general nodded brusquely before moving away to stand in studied isolation. He remained for a while, his head cocked to one side, almost as though sniffing the air. Then, after apparently nodding to himself, he rejoined Le Favre. 'Firing from the gunboats is easing off. I believe they've taken a bloody nose. So now it's the turn of their army, an' that Grant's a scrapper. He'll dish out more than our General Pillow can handle.' He paused momentarily to glance over at the prisoner. 'What do you think of his story, Captain?'

The officer proffered a sardonic smile. 'I'm inclined to think that half of what he says is lies, and the other half just plain ain't true. But. . . .'

Forrest's sharp laugh was almost a bark. 'Exactly. So, come the time I pull us out of this death-trap, he comes with us. Understand?'

It was pure happenstance that brought Frank Pootes into further contact with Ulysses S. Grant. The Union commander sat his mount on a low rise overlooking the advancing blue-coated troops. Members of his staff maintained a discreet distance. His keen eye spotted the two somewhat incongruous individuals moving against the flow.

'Still hunting your mysterious killers, Marshal?' he called out. 'Because there's any number of them around these parts.'

Pootes smiled and ascended the rise . . . on foot, of course. It was late afternoon, and he and Rhodes seemed to have been walking for an awful long stretch. Their time on the gunboat was just a distant memory. 'I can't leave without I give it my best. There's only two of them now, and we did actually catch up with one of the cockchafers, but sadly he got his self taken into yonder fortress by some rebel cavalry. But for this repeater, they'd like as not have got us as well.' He paused to get his breath before asking, 'Is there gonna be a big fight, General?'

Grant nodded slowly before disclosing far more than he normally would have done to a relative stranger. There was something about this resolute federal officer that impressed him. 'I think that there must be. Flag Officer Foote is sorely wounded and his ironclads were badly mauled, so we'll be obliged to put on a good show. Give those secessionists to understand that our intentions is serious. Then I'll serve them with an ultimatum.' He thought for a moment, before staring meaningfully at the lawman. 'If anyone intends breaking out of that fortress before it falls, then like as not it'll happen after they get my terms,' he added. 'And I'd put money on it being cavalry. It's unlikely they'd take any prisoners along for the ride, but then who knows?'

Since it had been horsemen that had captured his fugitive, the lawman immediately grasped the significance in that, but before he had chance to comment, Grant called out to a passing rider. 'Greetings, General. Perhaps you have encountered this peace officer before?'

Charles Ferguson Smith was, as usual with him,

leading his men from the front. His sharp glance took in Pootes and Rhodes. 'Harrumph,' he grunted. 'A civilian has no place on a battlefield. What happened to those two mounts I loaned you?'

'We kind of got separated, but they were in perfect health the last I saw of them,' Pootes replied, fully expecting a burst of expletives. What he got, along with everyone else, was a deafening roll of thunder, as the massed Union artillery opened fire behind them. Only the lawman seemed taken aback by the thunderous noise. Yet from then on, casual conversation was impossible, and so old General Smith merely proffered a salute to his superior before riding on.

Since the terrific bombardment showed no sign of abating, Pootes moved up to Grant's stirrup. 'Would you oblige me with the loan of two more horses, General? We might need to move fast, and my feet have been sorely tested.'

Grant, now drawing contentedly on a cigar as though he hadn't a care in the world, favoured him with a wry smile. 'I suppose that is little enough in the scheme of things,' he loudly retorted. 'I spy Captain Bragg approaching, and will instruct him to accommodate you.' And with that he was on the move again, constantly observing the progress of his army.

It occurred to Frank Pootes that there was at least one man fighting for the North who seemingly didn't entertain any thought of defeat.

*

Gideon Pillow was acutely nervous. Not just of the Union forces constantly hammering at his defences, but of General Forrest's reaction when that fearsome individual found out what his commanding officer had been up to. Because, although it had ended in a victory of sorts, the battle with the gunboats had badly shaken him. The fact that they had dared to come so close had graphically demonstrated the North's determination, and now their continued artillery bombardment only emphasized it. It was time to bow to the inevitable and prevent any further unnecessary deaths . . . especially his!

And so, having worked himself up to the premature conclusion that Fort Donelson was doomed, Pillow had sent an envoy through the lines under a flag of truce with a request for terms. And as the staff officer now rode back unharmed, it appeared as though he was about to get his reply. Impatiently, he waited in the headquarters building for the scrappy bit of paper to be placed in his hand. What it had to say left him staring disbelievingly at the hastily scribbled note.

No terms except an unconditional and immediate surrender can be accepted. I propose to move immediately upon your works.
Ulysses S. Grant. Commander of the Army of the Tennessee

Acutely conscious of the young officer standing curiously before him, Pillow struggled to control his emotions. He was stunned by the harsh and unchivalrous tone. So much so that he felt unwelcome tears welling up in his eyes. Yet there could be no help for it. Unconditional surrender it would have to be. And then, when he so desperately needed a moment to compose himself, General Forrest appeared, his face like thunder.

'Is it true? Have you asked for terms?'

Ashen-faced, and not trusting himself to speak, Pillow merely nodded.

'God damn you!' Forrest exclaimed. 'I did not come here for the purpose of surrendering my command.' For a moment it seemed as though he might strike his superior, but instead he turned and stalked off. Darkness was falling, and there wasn't a moment to waste.

Frank Pootes companionably hunkered down next to the sergeant in front of their small cooking fire, dunking army issue hardtack into piping hot coffee. It was jokingly said that the biscuit would stop bullets, and in its natural state was certainly proof against poorly maintained teeth.

Even though well clear of the massed artillery, there seemed to be no relief from the incessant detonations. Continuous muzzle flashes lit up the night sky in a beautiful but lethal display. Knowing that the Confederate defenders were seemingly on the point of surrender, Grant was deliberately keeping the pressure on.

The marshal gazed speculatively over the rim of

his coffee cup at the other man. 'If you were gonna sneak out of that fort tonight, Sam, which way would you go?'

The non-com thought for a moment. 'I'd take advantage of the darkness and use the trees by the river for cover.'

Pootes nodded. 'Makes sense to me. An' after what Grant said, I reckon we ought to get over there, pronto.'

Rhodes stared at him in surprise. 'What makes you think anyone making a break for it would take a no-account prisoner with them?'

Perhaps it was purely wishful thinking, on account of him having endured so much whilst attempting to apprehend his niece's killer, but Pootes was determined. 'It was cavalry that took him alive, when they could easily have shot him instead. And according to the general it'll likely be cavalry that attempts a breakout. I've no idea if the bastard will be with them, or even if he's still alive, but if he is then I need to be there. If it all comes to nought, then we'll just have to search for him in the fort when it falls.' He paused as though pondering something. 'If you want to sit this one out, I won't hold it agin you. You've more than pulled your weight in something that ain't really your fight.'

Even in the flickering light it was obvious that Sam Rhodes was deeply offended. 'That's a hell of a thing to say after what we've been through. I might have been assigned to you, but that pus weasel needs to answer for his bad deeds. So you ain't getting rid of me until the job's done and you head back up to Kentucky. Savvy?'

Pootes wasn't always an easy man to get along with, and knew it. Genuinely touched, he sighed heavily before replying, 'Yeah, yeah. I savvy. And don't pay me any heed, Sam. Sometimes I just got shit for brains, is all.' He paused for a moment as their eyes locked. 'So how's about we finish this business, *partner*?'

A slow smile spread over the sergeant's features. 'I reckon so.'

And so the two men got to their feet, kicked out the fire, and moved over to the ground-tethered horses. Whatever transpired that night, the two of them would face it together.

Despite his continued survival, Private Jason Metford had slipped into a veritable morass of misery and self-pity. He had again come to the conclusion that it was all that young bitch's fault up there in Kentucky, what with her tempting wiles and all. With his wrists still tightly manacled, he had been locked away in some kind of storage shack. There was noise aplenty, but the only light came from shell bursts and muzzle flashes. Occasionally a projectile came too close and showered the building with earth, which did little for his ragged nerves. Being encased in a uniform that was still damp and likely to remain that way, meant that his teeth were chattering uncontrollably. It seemed that if he didn't die from 'lead poisoning', then pneumonia would surely claim him.

How long he lay there, shivering despondently in the darkness, was beyond his comprehension. But then, quite suddenly, there was a clattering of bolts and the door was flung open. 'Get on your feet, you leach-lipped Yankee bastard,' a voice barked. 'You're going for a little ride'

Keen to be anywhere other than where he was, Metford gamely attempted to get off the ground, but his limbs failed him. That resulted in a brutal kick to his ribs that achieved nothing, because he was still unable to rise. Yet his predicament did attract the attention of higher authority.

'For Christ's sake, drag him out of there, Potts,' a harsh voice commanded. 'We're moving out, and the captain wants him mounted. . . without any ribs broke.'

Swearing fluently yet softly, Potts and another man heaved the prisoner to his feet and half carried him into the open. The feel of the cold night air on his flesh brought him to his senses a little, and then a tin cup was thrust into his right hand.

'Get that down you, bull turd,' someone hissed in his ear.

As hot coffee, heavily laced with strong liquor, flooded down Metford's throat, the voice added, 'Don't get to thinking we gone soft on you, Yankee. You've come down here to fight us, when we sure wouldn't have gone north to fight you. We just need you to stay in that saddle, is all.' So saying, strong hands hoisted him aloft, and reins were thrust into his left hand. At the same time, his boots were

140

rammed into waiting stirrups.

Still manacled and desperately clinging on to the cup, Metford greedily tipped the remaining contents down his gullet. His innards seemed to glow with a fiery warmth that spread outwards.

'Got any more of this?' he croaked hopefully.

By way of answer, the receptacle was roughly slapped out of his hand, and the horse began moving. 'You're roped to the animal in front,' yet another voice barked. 'So don't even think about trying to go off on your lonesome!'

And with that, they were off at speed into the night. Metford had no idea how many riders surrounded him, but one thing was for sure. He had absolutely no say over any of it!

CHAPTER ELEVEN

Any form of night-time action was habitually fraught with peril. Precious night vision, once lost, took minutes to recover, and, with artillery muzzle flashes still lighting up the sky, was likely to prove frustratingly elusive. It was also a fact that, with vast numbers of armed men on the move, lethal mistakes would occur.

The two horsemen moved cautiously away from the main body of the army and off to their left towards the river. Because of the continued presence of some of Foote's battered gunboats on the Cumberland, there were few infantry in the vicinity. It was a fact that Grant wasn't overly concerned about the possibility of rebels escaping. His main concern was possession of the fort and subsequent control of the watercourse leading into the Confederacy, rather than the accrual of prisoners that would require guarding. But that didn't mean that everyone the two manhunters encountered would be clad in butternut grey.

'Who all's out there?' a strangely disembodied voice abruptly bellowed out.

The two men momentarily froze, and then rapidly dismounted. Both took only vague aim with their rifles, because in truth neither of them had a firm target.

'Hold fire!' Rhodes commanded, before adding hopefully, 'We're with Grant, same as you.'

A distinctly slurred voice replied, 'That's bullshit. They ain't no federals twixt us and the fort.'

Before Rhodes could dispute that, first one and then a second shot rang out in the night. There was an audible thwack, as a large piece of lead slammed into flesh, and Pootes's mount gave a grunt of pain before keeling over. Incoherent hollering was followed by two further discharges, but there were no more casualties. Poor shooting from four men, and the sergeant believed he knew the reason why.

'God-damn bastards!' Pootes yelled, before charging straight for the source of the muzzle flashes. Even from his limited time with the Union army he well knew that unless he was unlucky enough to be confronted by cavalry equipped with Spencer repeating carbines, then the men facing him would be frantically reloading their single-shot Springfields.

With his blood well and truly 'up', the lawman pounded through the long grass. A few yards distant he made out a clutch of men. All were now on their feet so as to reload more easily, but to his eyes there appeared to be a powerful amount of fumbling going on. It seemed as though his latest mount had died through bad luck rather than any accuracy on their part. And then he spotted the reason. A large jug sat upright on the trampled grass. If that didn't contain bug juice he'd hand in his badge. Taking rapid aim, Pootes fired and was rewarded by the target smashing into a great many damp pieces. Levering in another cartridge, he fired again, kicking up dirt at the feet of the befuddled soldiers. *Union* soldiers!

Again working the under-lever, the marshal snarled, 'Ground those long guns, or I'll parole you all to Jesus!'

'Aw shit, mister!' one of them protested as he stared regretfully at the shattered whiskey jug. 'Why'd you have to go and do a thing like that?'

'Because General Grant himself gave me that horse, and you've just killed it,' Pootes retorted. 'Drop those guns!'

At that moment Rhodes joined him, his uniform and chevrons plain to see.

As the rifles were reluctantly grounded, another of the soldiers demanded, 'Just who the hell are you two, anyhu?'

The sergeant was scathing. 'You drunken no account trash. I'm with the 18th Illinois, an' you've just tried to kill a US marshal. You'll all hang for this!'

Such a drastic outcome was unlikely, but nevertheless a stunned silence fell on the group. They were sobering up fast, and weren't much enjoying the experience. But then came the sound of something even less appealing. Massed hoof beats clearly perceptible in the night. And whoever it was, they were coming directly towards the small band of Northerners!

Nathan Bedford Forrest reined his mount in slightly. Riding at the head of his men as always, he'd heard the cluster of shots up ahead. That in itself came as no surprise. They were on a battlefield, for Christ's sake. Yet such was his uncanny combat awareness that he had been able to differentiate between the discharges. And the final two closely spaced shots definitely hadn't come from any muzzle-loader!

The hairs tingled on the back of his neck as he rapidly considered his options. To veer to the left would take his brigade towards the main Union forces. To his right lay oak trees and the river, cutting down on their manoeuvrability and taking him in range of any gunboats still out there. So continuing straight ahead was his only real choice. And with close to a thousand men at his back, they should be able to sweep through anything that awaited them.

'Cavalry coming this way can only mean one thing,' Sam Rhodes opined. 'It's rebs breaking out.'

'And therefore very likely our last chance of catching 'powder burn', *if* he's still alive,' Pootes remarked, before glancing at their four 'prisoners'. Suddenly everything had changed. 'The ground ain't no place for your firearms,' he snapped. 'Pick 'em up and make ready. There's a fight coming!'

145

Even in the indifferent light, he couldn't fail to spot the sheer horror on their grubby, unshaven features. Every one of them was now stone-cold sober.

'Jesus, mister!' one of the soldiers exclaimed. 'Sounds to me like there's an awful lot of them manure spreaders. We'll get chewed up for sure.'

That cut no ice with Sergeant Rhodes. 'You miserable skunk. You was happy enough to pop a cap on us.'

'That was the "who hit John" talking,' the private protested. 'We weren't ourselves then,'

'Well, now you are, an' you're gonna make a goddamn stand with us or I'll shoot you myself.' He tapped the chevrons on his sleeve. 'And that's an order.'

The approaching body of horsemen began to materialize in the gloom, proving that the reluctant soldier was correct in one respect. There *were* an awful lot of them!

'Don't bother with any fancy shooting,' Pootes instructed. If he had known just how many of the enemy there really were out there he would probably have reconsidered. As it was, only part of the column was visible, and so he added, 'Just aim at the mass of them and keep firing. Me and this Henry'll cover your reloading. Do it!'

And such was the force behind his words that they did just that.

General Forrest just happened to be looking off to his left when a ragged volley crashed out in the gloom. Against such a closely packed target, their assailants couldn't miss, and they didn't. As usual it was the unfortunate animals that took the brunt. Cries and grunts rang out in the night, as both horses and riders tumbled to the ground, tripping up some of those following behind. Because the men under Forrest's command were already tested veterans, chaos reigned for only a very brief period. The general had counted a mere five muzzle flashes, which in itself was puzzling. Why would they be foolish enough to take on such vastly superior numbers? It made no sense. And yet he couldn't allow them to continue shooting unchallenged as the rest of his men passed by.

'You'd best deal with them, Captain Le Favre,' he barked at the nearest officer. 'And make it quick. We need to be gone from here, so don't let it turn into something it shouldn't.'

After saluting his acknowledgement, that man yelled out his orders and then swung away from the brigade followed by approximately fifty men. In the heat of the moment, neither he nor his commander had recalled the fact that the captain was also responsible for their single Union prisoner, tagging along near the rear. And as another volley crashed out he had other things on his mind. Three more animals suffered grievous wounds, but this time only they and their riders fell, because the horsemen were far more widely spread.

'Charge the bastards,' Le Favre hollered. 'Don't give them chance to reload.' He could now clearly make out five individuals frenetically tipping powder and lead down the barrels of their rifles. Despite the casualties, the officer smiled, because he knew full well that the infantrymen, out in the open without any available cover, wouldn't manage another volley. Although armed with a revolver, he chose instead to draw and point his sabre. Impaling a hated invader on it did far more damage than slashing with the edge and was much more satisfying than using a firearm.

With pounding hoofs, the cavalry detachment rapidly closed in on the apparently defenceless Yankee invaders. Gleefully they let rip with the famous Rebel yell, a cross between a hunting yip and a howl, which was most times guaranteed to give pause to any enemy. But then something strange happened. A solitary individual stepped out from behind the others and levelled a weapon. There was a flash and one of the Confederates fell stricken from his horse. And then, horrifyingly, that wasn't the end of it. A lethal stream of lead continued to tear into the charging horsemen, catching them completely off guard. The breathtaking speed of the shots was faster than any Spencer or revolver could manage . . . and they just kept on coming. And whatever the weapon was, its owner sure knew how to use it. More victims crashed to the ground until the still vastly superior force instinctively pulled away. As a consequence, the Confederate rear became briefly visible, and with it their captive.

*

Even in the poor light, Frank Pootes caught sight of the manacled rider and intuitively realized who it must be. He swung his Henry over, but at that instant one of the downed rebels leapt to his feet and raced towards him brandishing a sabre. Cursing bitterly, the marshal adjusted his aim and fired. The bullet slammed into the running man, knocking him off his feet, this time permanently. Desperately working the under-lever, Pootes again took aim at the prisoner's horse. The distance was rapidly growing. In such conditions he would only get the one chance. Yet he never doubted his ability. The lawman squeezed the trigger, to be rewarded with only a metallic click. Empty!

For a brief moment his spirits sank lower than hammered shit. To fail now after all that he had gone through was just too cruel. Then a voice at his side muttered, 'I got the bastard!'

Sam Rhodes had his Springfield levelled. He inhaled, held his breath and fired. The recoil told him that his Minie bullet was in flight, but for a frustrating moment the acrid smoke prevented him from seeing the result.

Jason Metford had never felt so utterly helpless in his life, especially as he thought that he knew the identity of at least one of those shooting at them. Securely manacled and all the while being pulled hither and thither on a fast-moving horse, he could only pray that they might ride like the wind away from the ambuscade before a piece of lead found its way to him. And then it happened. Something must have

149

struck his mount, because the creature stumbled in mid step and never recovered. With great force, Metford was flung from his saddle and on to the long grass. Although the growth slightly cushioned his fall, the wind was still knocked from his lungs. To make matters worse, the man who had been leading him was yanked from his saddle and came tumbling down on top, pinning him to the ground. With the Confederate cavalry fast departing, the two fallen men were abruptly quite alone.

'Cover me, Sam,' Pootes instructed, as he hurriedly slipped fresh cartridges down into the tubular magazine. 'I mean to make me an arrest. You others watch out for those sons of bitches coming back.'

Only when they had both reloaded did he venture towards the two prone figures. As they cautiously approached, one of the men suddenly rolled on to his side and pointed some kind of weapon. Pootes didn't hesitate. He fired three shots in rapid succession, working the under-lever like a berserker. His victim jerked three times under impact and then lay still. The lawman fervently hoped that it wasn't 'powder burn', because he fully intended to see that man dangle at the end of a rope after the due process of law had been observed.

'Shit, but that's some gun,' Rhodes opined yet again as they closed in on the lone survivor. 'It's way faster than any Spencer.'

'You reckon?' Pootes muttered with just a hint of sarcasm.

Before the sergeant could respond, they reached the two human forms. One was soaked in blood and quite obviously dead. The other, who was painfully drawing breath, abruptly turned to scrutinize them. Still manacled, he appeared to present little threat, but Pootes told his companion to keep his Springfield on him anyway.

That man nodded and then yelled back to the four infantrymen. 'Remember what the marshal done told you. Keep your eyes peeled for any more of those Johnny Rebs. I seen your faces now, so no one run out on us.'

Pootes, meanwhile, had knelt down for a better look at the prisoner. As he took in the powder burn under Metford's right eye, he suddenly felt real anger building inside. Not the casual anger against someone trying to kill him in battle or resisting arrest, but real rage for the savage treatment of a dear relative. And yet he had no intention of succumbing to it. This would be done legal.

'You're under arrest,' he snarled.

'For what?'

The marshal drew in a steadying breath. 'For the rape and murder of Miss Martha Pootes of Christian County, Kentucky. My niece. And also the attempted murder of a federal officer. That's me.'

Metford regarded the other's baleful expression speculatively for a moment before fatalistically deciding there was little point in denying anything. So if his captor had been hoping for some show of repentance, he was to be sadly disappointed. 'Yeah, well,' he rasped. 'Truth is, I right enjoyed it . . . law dog. The raping, anyhu. That little missy was ripe as a peach.'

A red mist seemed to envelop Pootes's eyes. It was only with a tremendous effort of will that he didn't squeeze the Henry's trigger, to end it there and then. Instead, he slammed the butt into Metford's belly, taking grim satisfaction from the groan of pain that it induced. Then he recalled something. 'I already know about the fella whose throat you slit, but what happened to the other bastard that was with you? Tell me, or so help me God I'll shoot your other ear off.'

Metford's whole body was wracked with pain. He had no reason to hold back. 'Got his head blowed off on that gunboat,' he gasped.

Pootes shook his head. So the Pittsburgh's captain had at least been partly telling the truth. 'Help me get this piece of trash on his feet,' he ordered through gritted teeth. 'Before I misremember the oath I took.'

The two men seized their suffering captive under his armpits and heaved. It was at that moment that they again heard the pounding of hoofs.

Nathan Bedford Forrest might have been a general of brigade, but he always led from the front, or was present wherever the greatest danger happened to be. So it was that, with the majority of his men safely out of range, he waited to ensure that Le Favre's detachment arrived back safely. Even in the gloom he could see that their numbers were reduced. And there was something else as well. The manacled Yankee was nowhere in sight. The fact that he should not have even accompanied them would have to be addressed later.

'Where the hell is my prisoner, Captain?' he demanded.

That officer had the good grace to be embarrassed. 'I can only assume that he has been taken, sir.'

Since there wasn't time for recriminations, Forrest merely glowered at him. Such a reaction spoke volumes and boded ill. Then, as was so typical of the fighting general, he withdrew the LeMat from its flap holster and savagely dug his heels in. The most extraordinary feature of his unique sidearm was the single, twenty-gauge shotgun barrel positioned within the rotating cylinder and under the normal revolver barrel. This could deliver a devastating blow when used at close quarters, which was where he usually found himself in any scrap.

Oblivious as to whether any of his men followed him or not, he took off at a gallop towards the Union skirmishers. In the dark, and on uncertain ground, such speed was reckless to be sure, but Forrest was a natural predator with one very specific aim in mind. Clutching the reins in one hand and his massive revolver in the other, he rapidly retraced the trail taken by the badly mauled detachment. The fact that all those men had been put to flight, and yet he was returning alone never entered his thoughts.

With the Cumberland on his left, the general

came sweeping out of the night like an avenging demon. Ahead of him were three distinctive forms. Two of them appeared to flank the third, but whether they were assisting him or restraining him could not be immediately discerned. Since successfully killing them all at once was a tall order, there was only one thing for it. Swinging his animal to the left, he began a rapid circuit of the startled Yankees.

Having apparently seen off the rebel cavalry, Frank Pootes's heart jolted with shock at the sight of a single horseman pounding directly for them. As the lone rider came closer, the marshal released his hold on Metford. Armed with a vastly superior weapon, it made good sense for him to handle the threat. Tucking the Henry into his shoulder, he took rapid aim at their fast-approaching foe. His forefinger tightened just at the very moment that the speeding figure executed a sharp turn.

The rifle crashed out, but its target was no longer there. Cursing the man's apparently uncanny prescience, Pootes worked the under-lever and again desperately attempted to bring the muzzle to bear. At the same time he got his first proper glimpse of their solitary assailant. From his flamboyant style of dress he was an officer to be sure, and one that even at speed seemed to project an extraordinary malevolence. Although all alone, he was circling them in the same fashion as a tribe of marauding plains Indians surrounding a wagon train of settlers. This was definitely no ordinary man!

Having avoided the first projectile, Forrest held the LeMat ready on his right side as he sped around the three Yankees. He was searching for something specific, and as the moonlight momentarily glinted on metal 'bracelets' he knew he'd found it.

Metford trembled with sheer horror as he saw the revolver line up on his torso. At his side, Rhodes struggled to get clear of him and raise his long-barrelled rifle. Very briefly he wondered why the four infantrymen didn't open fire. The answer to that, of course, was that they had fled at the first sound of more hoof beats.

'For Christ's sake do something?' Metford wailed as he struggled against his shackles. All movement seemed to be occurring in slow motion . . . except for those of the looming attacker. The horseman was before him for barely an instant, but it was long enough.

With a tremendous flash, the lower barrel erupted, throwing a lethal charge of shot directly into Metford's chest. Under the terrible impact, flesh and muscle were quite literally torn to shreds. He endured a fleeting moment of indescribable agony, and then there was only oblivion. All that remained was for his body to involuntarily twitch through its death throes. And so, by a glorious twist of fate, the murderer's own lies had effectively brought about his bloody demise.

As the now dead weight fell away from Rhodes's grasp, General Forrest closed the circle and bellowed out, 'If I can't have him, you sure ain't about to,

Pinkerton man!' Then, expertly zigzagging his animal, he sped away. Sheer exhilaration animated his normally grim features. At least now the Yankees wouldn't know whether their deserter had divulged Grant's secrets or not. All that remained was for him to get safely out of range. Yet even someone of Forrest's astonishing ability couldn't outrun a bullet.

'What the Sam Hill was that all about?' the bewildered sergeant gasped. 'He looked like the devil himself.'

Ignoring him, Pootes drew a bead on the fleeing man's broad back and his finger again tightened on the trigger. Despite the desperate evasive action, he felt sure that he could claim a kill if he so chose. And yet something stopped him. Although an enemy, that fellow American had, by acting as judge, jury and executioner, just saved him a great deal of trouble. Perhaps then it was only right and proper that that extraordinary individual should live to fight another day. Nodding to himself, he lowered his rifle and eased the hammer down.

The marshal, who like many Northerners still thought that it would be a short war, couldn't possibly have envisaged that Nathan Bedford Forrest would return to haunt the Union time and time again!

CHAPTER TWELVE

'So you've ended up with a corpse rather than a prisoner.' It was a statement rather than a question, and as he uttered it, Ulysses S. Grant, or Unconditional Surrender Grant as he was now known, favoured the lawman with a quizzical glance. The victorious general, having vanquished both Fort Henry and Donelson, appeared uncharacteristically presentable in his freshly brushed uniform. He was soon to have his image captured, supposedly forever, by the remarkable modern process of photography. A wagon containing myriad chemicals and plates owned by a certain George Bernard, in the employ of the celebrated Mathew Brady, had recently rattled through the pickets with the intention of recording the war in the mid west. Even the relatively unsophisticated Grant could see the likely benefit of having his name and picture in the newspapers back east.

Frank Pootes proffered a genuine smile. There could be no doubt that this rough and ready general had a certain charisma, but then wasn't that always the case with successful people? Somewhat guardedly, he produced a leather pouch from a pocket. 'Actually I've made do with a pair of ears. I reckon I need to show my brother something for his loss, and a cadaver wouldn't travel well over the time it'll take to get back up to LaFayette.'

Grant laughed out loud at the gruesome revelation. 'You're a man after my own heart, Marshal.'

'Maybe so, but I'm still glad this man was kilt by a rebel. After all, murdering rapist or not, he *was* a soldier in the Union Army, and questions could have been asked.'

'Not by me, and it's *my* army,' Grant gruffly replied. 'Goodbye, Marshal Pootes. It's been a pleasure making your acquaintance.'

The two men companionably sat their horses on a bluff overlooking the Cumberland River and close to the captured fortress. All around them was a hive of activity, as steamboats arrived from Cairo with reinforcements and much needed supplies. The Army of the Tennessee (River) would soon be moving on, and Grant was being recognized with grudging admiration as a 'push hard'. There was even talk that he might be rewarded with a promotion to major general. President Lincoln, damnably frustrated by George McClellan's interminable delays and excuses back east, always looked favourably on anyone prepared to fight for his cause.

The sergeant in particular was in no all-fired hurry

to break the contemplative mood. He well knew that when Pootes released him from duty, he would have to surrender his horse and return to being a footsore infantryman once again, and he had kind of taken to his elevated role. Sadly though, that moment was not far off. Rhodes's next remark was therefore intended to delay the inevitable, but actually achieved the opposite result.

'How's your brother gonna take it, when he doesn't get to see the rest of the body? After all, that cockchafer did kill his only daughter, an' kin can be funny about such things.' Even whilst uttering the words, he had painfully recognized that he hadn't conveyed his meaning very well.

Frank Pootes glanced over at him sharply. 'He'll see what he's given, 'cause I sure ain't digging that poxy bastard up agin.' He paused for a moment. 'You know something? I never did find out his God-damned name. And of course if I'd known that Bernard fella was going to roll into camp, I'd have maybe had him take a likeness. But then happen he'll be too busy with generals and the like.' He suddenly patted the pocket containing his macabre trophies and added, 'As it is, I reckon these'll just have to tell the tale.'

The lawman's expression abruptly softened. Talk of his brother reminded him that it was past time to be on his way, which meant that the moment had arrived to say his goodbyes, and he felt strangely choked up at the prospect. This non-com had obviously grown on him, because he smiled and unexpectedly blurted out, 'You're real fine people, Sergeant.'

'Thank you kindly, *Frank*,' Rhodes replied, matching the other's smile. 'I'd have to allow, you ain't such a bad cuss yourself.'

Pootes thrust out his hand, which was gladly accepted. 'Well then, it seems like my work here is done. I'm off back to Kentucky, away from all this madness. Where to for you?'

The sergeant shrugged. As always in the army he could never fully trust what he'd been told. 'Cap'n says we're making for somewhere called Shiloh. Has a nice gentle ring to it, don't it? Apparently it means place of peace, so let's hope it stays that way!'